MAZE OF BLOOD

MAZE OF BLOOD

A NOVEL

MARLY·YOUMANS

MERCER UNIVERSITY PRESS · MACON, GEORGIA

MUP/H905

© 2015 by Mercer University Press
Published by Mercer University Press
1400 Coleman Avenue
Macon, Georgia 31207
All rights reserved

9 8 7 6 5 4 3 2 1

Books published by Mercer University Press are
printed on acid-free paper that meets the requirements
of the American National Standard for Information Sciences—
Permanence of Paper for Printed Library Materials.

Book design by Mary-Frances Burt / Burt&Burt

Illustrations by Clive Hicks-Jenkins

ISBN 978-0-88146-536-5

Cataloging-in-Publication Data is available from the Library of Congress

for Laura Murphy Frankstone and Jeffery Beam

*I thought of a maze of mazes, of a sinuous, ever growing maze
which would take in both past and future
and would somehow involve the stars.*

—Jorge Luis Borges, "The Garden of Forking Paths"

Acknowledgments

Maze of Blood was drafted during a residence at
Yaddo in 2007. I thank The Yaddo Foundation and
its staff for quiet, time, and a room of my own.

While fiction, *Maze of Blood* was inspired by the life
of pulp writer Robert E. Howard. Secondary sources
essential to me were *One Who Walked Alone* by
Novalyne Price Ellis; *Blood & Thunder* by Mark
Finn; and *Two-Gun Con: A Centennial Study of
Robert E. Howard.*

Poems quoted are from Samuel Taylor Coleridge.

MᴀZE ᴏf BLOOD

The Maze of Youth

·

Child in the Bloodroot Maze

·

The Soul, the Spirit, and the Meteorite

MAZE OF BLOOD

Texas Curtain-Raiser

Studded with corpses that looked like raisins, a fly tape hung over his head. He stared at it. Strange how a thing so light could be so absolutely still. *The heft of death,* he supposed. *Heft.* He liked that, thought about writing a poem but lay in the tangle of sheets, prisoned in swelter like a bug in amber.

Close by a rooster strutted about the world, vocalizing for the benefit of the neighborhood, proud of having made the sun boil up and swarm over the edge of the state, igniting the plains and lowlands and panhandle. *Thinks the sun comes up just to hear him crow.* That was one of Doc's sayings. Somebody must be moving about the kitchen because now he could hear the spit of frying grease. He stirred abruptly and then lay still, feeling a wash of prickly heat. Dots of perspiration formed above his lip.

What did you need of hell when you had Texas?

The dawn glare shoved slantwise through the windows, striking and illuminating motes of dust in the air.

Texas really was hell without your dog, without your girl. *Caradog ap Bran. Maybelline. Both gone.* No wonder he had been wandering in his thoughts, lying awake since before light, daydreaming his death, running and climbing to meet it.

Why, he had the whole weight of the Lone Star State on his back like some kind of crazy sheriff's badge, big as a millstone—all those Texans with their tidy lives, their distrust of stories not like their own.

What if you brought the people tales like stolen fire, but nobody cared? What if the fire changed to ashes in your burned hands?

He hated them for a moment, tensing against the whole realm with its rickracked aprons and locust posts joined up with barbed wire. *Frankenstein state*, he thought, *the whole place patchworked together out of scraps and flesh and crazy quilt stitches.*

Everything might have been different if he had gone away, but he hadn't, somehow couldn't go. And yet he couldn't bear to become the little thing people here wanted him to be. Well, there was no use festering over it. He wouldn't be small. They couldn't make him.

"Rankles," he said in a low voice. "It rankles."

The night when a meteorite swept from the sky and punched into the earth swam into his memory, barely visible like a scene beheld through heat waves over macadam. He remembered a stink that he imagined to be like the old-timey lucifer matches, the light flashing around him, and the tumble out the window, so quick! At once the little boy he had been grasped that the world was terribly big, terribly strange and savage.

"Hell, if I'd never seen that meteor," he said to the raisins on the fly tape, "maybe everything would have been different." The thought made his mouth quirk into an off-kilter smile.

"Conall! Breakfast!"

His stomach growled, and he swung his legs to the floor, pushing away the damp caul of sheets. It didn't seem fair, he thought, that a place so hot and dry wanted its people to sweat— wanted to suck the moisture right out of them. No wonder they were left as hard as their fence posts sometimes. He could already tell the day would be a scorcher.

"Be there in a minute," he called.

The light outside increased.

Battalions. Spears. The soldiery light trying to break into the body...

His black pants, draped over the back of a chair, looked stiff and uncomfortable. He sat on the bed to pull them on, daydreaming about armor forged from light.

The Maze of Ashes

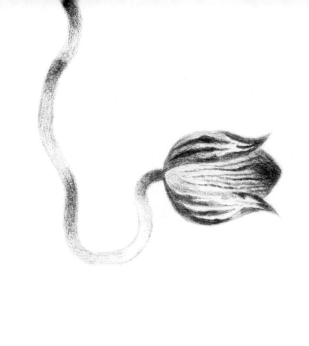

The Velvet Bouquet

"I don't know what's gotten into you." Doc chortled and drew a thin muslin handkerchief from his pants pocket. He dabbed at the corners of his mouth. "Do you know what Conall's gone and done, Mama? He's tossed out that sorry old bouquet."

"Is that right?" Maeve twisted her head to look at where it had been. Nothing. "It was ugly, wasn't it? Just got uglier and uglier." She leaned against the sun-faded couch, her head on the antimacassar. She had lost forty pounds and looked gaunt in the face and arms.

Doc was patting his eyes with the handkerchief.

"I threw it away," Conall said. "I just couldn't stand how it looked for another instant."

"What did you do with the base and the dome?" Maeve looked again, as if the flowers might still be there, their purpose abandoned but still standing quietly under a fine sprinkle of dust.

"I threw them away, too."

"Well, that's too bad," she said. "You could have put something else under there, couldn't you?"

"No, ma'am," he said. "I couldn't put a damn thing on show that way."

"No need to say 'damn' about a poor little dome of glass and a base."

"Yes, ma'am."

"Nobody liked it, Mama. That bunch of flowers wasn't doing anybody a scrap of good." Doc laughed again and rubbed his eyes. He had been up to all hours with a woman having a baby and afterward invited himself to stay and eat breakfast with the family.

"That bouquet sure was a sad sight," she admitted. "It's been a long time since the day we got married. I can't remember who gave us that present, and seems like the flowers were a different color back then."

"They were purple. It was all right. Just a toy for grown folks." Doc shook out his handkerchief and then folded it into a small square. "How'd you go about the disposal, son?"

Conall's eyebrows lifted. "You want to know how I threw it away?"

"Well, in the burn barrel, I guess, except for the glass," his mother said.

"No, ma'am," Conall said. "I took it up to Caddo Peak East, and I set it upright on a rotten tree stump, and then I shot the thing to pieces."

"Well, of all the—why'd you do that?" His father pushed his glasses up onto the bridge of his nose and stared. "Why in tarnation—"

"Maybe I wanted to be Kubla Kahn. 'I would build that dome in air, / That sunny dome! those caves of ice.'" Conall's laugh was short, choked-off. "Just felt like it. I just felt like shooting that thing all to hell."

"Pretty strange," the old man muttered.

"Boys like to shoot," his mama said, "and Conall has always liked going to either of the Caddo Peaks. Isn't that right? He'd come home with a hat piled high with the fossils of sea creatures."

"Which gun did you use? You didn't ask me for a key to the lockbox."

His father stared at him, frowning, waiting for the mystery to clear.

"I borrowed a Colt .38 off Fletcher. Blew the flowers to smithereens. See this cut?" He pointed to a thin, jagged line of red on his cheek. "I was standing too close. Had to pick glass out of my chest. I should've expected that, but I wasn't thinking straight."

"I'll be," Doc said.

"I took it into my head somehow. It was last week when Mama was so sick, and I was up all night with her three nights. Seemed like every time I got her soaked gown dragged off and a dry one on, she broke out in another sweat. Finally we ran out of gowns and I had to wrap her up in sheets. Then when you came by the house, I decided to light out. I needed some air. And just grabbed up the bouquet as I left." He laughed, remembering how the whim had seized him.

"Guess that's one way to get rid of it," his father said uneasily. "Mama, I'm afraid Conall's doing too much. Maybe I ought to cut back on the practice for a while."

"And how would you do that, I wonder?" Asperity tinged Maeve's words. "You wouldn't want to neglect a patient."

"I don't know, but maybe—did you just climb up with it in your arms, son, or what?"

"I had it tucked under my elbow like a football, and the Colt in my back pocket with the hammer down." Conall leaned forward to demonstrate how he had held the glass and stand.

"So you went up there and just tore it to bits."

"The first blast sent glass flying and caught the bouquet smack in the middle." Conall punched the air with his fist. "The velvet was so old and dry that it exploded into little tatters. It was like something that had been dead for years. But the wood took four shots to kill. I buried the scraps in a hole in the limestone."

"Why?" His father took off his glasses, cleaned them on his handkerchief, and then put them back on. "Why do it?"

Conall shrugged. "Just needed to let off steam, maybe. 'The vicissitudes of existence,' as Louÿs says, were cramping me."

"Are you all right now?"

"Of course, he's fine. He's just worn down." His mother patted the arm of the couch. "He's a good boy."

"Sure. When I got home, I took a rag and cleaned the table. There was a perfect circle where it had been sitting, surrounded by dust."

Doc gazed at him and then gave a quick nod of the head. "Fair enough. I was worried that all this caretaking had got you worked up."

"No, sir. Seems like you told me once that a man does what he has to do, but sometimes he needs to break out a little and run around the pasture."

Maeve's head lolled to the side. She had fallen asleep. Her flyaway white hair stood up in a cockscomb and caught the sunlight, and her face was pale save for the darkness in her half-open mouth that looked like a black smile.

"It's a damn pitiful shame," Conall said, watching her. "She's got close to nothing left."

"She's not doing too bad, considering," Doc said.

"You think so?"

His father fumbled with the glasses and handkerchief again, complaining that he couldn't see a damn thing through scratched-up lenses.

"Well, I'm going to my room. Thought I'd put my tales in order, get organized. They're an awful mess."

"All right, son. You go right ahead. I'm glad to see you getting work done."

"I'm not doing anything new. Just tidying up. I can't get anything accomplished right now."

Conall shambled off to the converted porch, where he sat on the edge of the bed. Eventually he lay back, staring at the ceiling. He had told his father a lie. His papers were already arranged, each story carefully clipped to a carbon copy with a note about where to submit. Although a faint wish that he would feel the desire to read or write came to him, he did not move.

There's not a drop left in the well, he thought. The words had simply slipped away, and he would never again revel in their glory and magic. He knew that he had done so in the past, but he couldn't feel even the least sparkle of those hours of writing—the lost time when stories had let him live in a world where acts had meaning. Without the words, his days felt like some endless limbo, all perdition and Texas heat.

Now he couldn't seem to get away from Texas even in his dreams. Only the night before Conall had found himself wandering in the fenced back lot, though he hadn't walked in his sleep in a long time. He was so weary that he couldn't seem to catch up on his rest, and in the small hours of the night he started awake in a panic, his heart beating too quickly and a roaring in his ears. Strong as he was, he often felt like just-poured liquid trembling in a glass.

It's done. Everything except the vow to take care of her. Because who would wring out her gowns and bathe her body and see to everything properly if I left? Doc just wouldn't be here.

There wasn't much he could do, anyway, because TB was bigger than any medical man. Besides, a doctor didn't want to hear about sickness and patients once he got done with his rounds. Perhaps that was part of the reason his father had never really liked being home.

"Freedom," he whispered. Ahead of him was a life without the tethers that had long held him, or so his friend Fletcher said.

Conall felt dizzy. He turned over on his side and crushed the pillow around his head. All he wanted was to bury himself in slumber. He didn't even have the desire to wake refreshed. His wish was for oblivion to blot out the invisible darkness that moved with him as he moved.

No longer did he think about returning to the world in a millennium to come or about flying to the world tree to nest and sing until it was time for a new life. Even that life as a bird-soul seemed too wearisome to contemplate. He had ceased to dream its flights, so the bird vanished.

Nor did he remember past lives with Genghis Khan or Vortigern. He no longer wandered Atlantis in a daydream, its mazy tangle of streets leading to mysteries. Sometimes it seemed that he had never lived or loved at all, neither now nor then. The drab freight of nothingness pressed him, driving out all story.

In the end, he thought, *a neat labyrinth or an untidy maze is a place that is simple. You reach its heart and are devoured by the beast, or you reach its heart and the spot is absolutely bare and pulseless. Maybe the beast and the blankness are the same. Maybe it is the emptiness that has teeth and hollows you out.*

You can deck a maze in colors. You can even make the walls from tatters of tubercular lung or panels like frozen blood.

But it doesn't change what is changeless.

Betrayal

An edge of anger livened him.

It woke the flickering images that stretched through thousands of years into the past—his inheritance, the seeds of his stories. They were all different, yet through each ran a scarlet Ariadne's thread that perhaps could lead him out of the corridors that closed in around him.

Maybelline.

He had gone so far, even said that he was willing to try and be what he thought Maybelline wanted him to be, an ordinary fellow. For her he was willing to give up wearing his boxing pants a bit short, the way he liked them. Really, you never knew when you might need to fight, and the wrong clothes could hold you back, cost you. Both boxers and Texas farmers needed their pants cut high.

Why, he had offered to venture into the town and perhaps even to the school to see her plays, if that's what she wanted. He hated it that she wanted to be a teacher, that she had almost given up the idea of being a writer, but he would have done whatever she asked. She had wanted him—wanted to marry him. Hadn't they joked about it?

He had even declared that he would put on his brown suit and go to church with her on Sunday. Perhaps he could come to an understanding with Old Yahweh, he had said—something like that. No, he wouldn't mind drinking the milk of Paradise! Twice a day he milked the cow in the shed out back. He would milk the great crystal cow with its eye like a star and the burning wreath looped around its head. A pail full of heaven's cream could do a writer no harm, if Old Yahweh would give him leave to drink. When he thought of church, his mind always went straight to the Old Testament God because He held the javelins and lightning bolts of power as a sheaf in His right hand. Authority and mystery. Mystery was something to admire, at least if it refused to give up all its secrets, but how Conall hated authority! Even as a small child, he smoldered inwardly at the way he was hemmed in by other people's rules.

Yes, he loved Maybelline and was willing to give up all his feathered twigs of mystery for her sake—to put down the arrows and be a common man.

"I was drawn to you because you were extraordinary," she had said. "Nothing could take that away. Wearing a shirt and tie with pants that aren't halfway to a little boy's short pants wouldn't make you one of the herd."

Was she laughing at him then?

She sure as hell was laughing at him now.

All those clues came down like yellow leaves, one by one, until the bare skeleton of truth shone out, a dead tree lit up by a wink of lightning. He remembered wondering whether she didn't care for his friend Fletcher because she always veered on to some other subject when the name came up. Once she saw the two friends together and turned to walk the other way. But he didn't understand the signs until he picked up a book one afternoon with a message from Fletcher on the flyleaf. That a book should provide the message of betrayal!

A book, a love, a friend: all had left him alone in a tubercular house of blood with no exit.

Hadn't she even turned his own words and sayings on him, hardened and sharpened the syllables and plunged them into his heart? She reminded him that he was a cowboy and that cowboys ride alone. Why, a woman would take that lasso and tie the poor cowboy down!

She even reminded him that a few spoonfuls of native blood ran in her veins and that his mother didn't like Indians. Why did he tell her Maeve's words, she had asked, if he didn't want her to know that his mother refused her? Wasn't he always writing about the cataclysmic smash-up between peoples? She was a mongrel smash-up all on her own!

Yes, he had said the things that she turned into weapons against him. That much was true. And yes, he had told her that a man who followed his dream to finality was alone and needed neither a god nor a companion.

But he had said so many other things! A man couldn't be just one thing, could he? Only a fool said the same words all the time. Hadn't he told her in a thousand ways that she was his best girl— the girl for this and every other millennium since the start of this evil world that reeled between civilization and barbarism but never got an inch or an ounce more worthy?

Fletcher.

To be betrayed by his close friend! It was intolerable, though perhaps he had feared and dimly foreseen that such could happen in this and every other lifetime.

Perhaps some impulse made Maybelline go with Fletcher one day when the two met by accident—if anything in this treacherous life was accident. Perhaps when she was with another man, she came to realize Conall's strangeness. Perhaps she saw that he was painfully askew, slaunchways from the rest of the world.

What was there to say about such a betrayal? In the glove box of his car lay the Colt .38 he had used to blow the glass dome to pieces. He could not bring himself to drive over to where Fletcher was living now and hand him the borrowed gun, though it had occurred to him that his friend might be frightened, seeing him fling open the picket gate and stride up the yard with a weapon in his hand. No, he would let somebody else return the gun.

Still, that might have been an interesting moment to create.

Once they had been playmates in the back lot where his dog was buried. One day Maeve had tied dishtowels on their heads for pirate kerchiefs and strung a leaf on a string for each, to serve as an eye patch. Their pirate ship was a big wooden packing crate with a torn bedspread flung across the door. The boys scratched the soil into a maze of waterways and islands, outlined with sticks.

Conall remembered feeling a swell of gladness. His father had bought this house and meant to settle down at last. They would not be moving again.

How had all that good feeling ebbed away?

Later on, people were startled by his choices. What had begun with surprise, Conall felt, ended in rejection. They scorned him for playing with words instead of doing a man's work, whether it was pulling cotton or adding up columns of figures or amputating a foot with gangrene. The proper citizens of the bugtussle realm of Texas could not accept the idea of somebody clinging to beauty and art instead of a cash register. He made good money at his yarns, too, but the ditch-digging men couldn't stand that either. Couldn't respect a fellow who used his mind and heart and soul instead of brute force.

Instead of being beloved for bringing wordsmithing to the prairie, he became the village idiot. He had heard the japes. *Boy's studying to be a halfwit. Feather merchant. Snakes in the clabber. Mind like an armadillo rodeo.*

"My bosh," he called his stories, defensive and shamed.

Maybelline thought that he had dug his own grave, but she was wrong.

There had been happy times, he was sure of it, if he could only find them in the corridors of the past. His thoughts ran back to the game of pirates on the back lot. He and Fletcher had yelled and pounded across the earth and never tired. The two of them had sunk the ships of the pirate queen and carried off her treasures of crystal and gold, hiding them for safekeeping in a chest made from a cigar box.

Once he had turned a cartwheel and stood up, rocking on his heels. At that very instant a gust had bowled yellow leaves across the ground, and Caradog, his ears blown back from his head like the two wings on the helmet of Hermes, vaulted high, high into the air and snatched a leaf in his jaws while the two boys leaped in the wind, shouting with surprise and joy.

A King in Cross Plains

"No shadows," the king said, wincing at the flood of Texas sunshine that blanched the room.

"At noon, the light's stark and unbearable," Conall said. "Later, the shadows jump out and are sharp as knife blades. There's a lot of sun and a lot of sky and a lot of flat land for shadows to run along."

Brennus, ruler of the Picts, was sweating under his wolfskin cloak.

"That's not what you wanted to say," he observed, sitting down in a rocker but starting to his feet again as it swayed under his weight. He pushed the arms hard and watched the chair pitch back and forth. After it slowed, he sat again, his face touched by a rare smile. He rocked slowly at first and then vigorously. The cloak, hanging over the top rail of the rocker, flapped against the spindles.

"I'm thinking about taking my own life. I've been thinking about it for a long time."

The king stopped his rocking.

"Taking?"

"Killing."

"Killing your own life?" Brennus began rocking again, more slowly this time. "Can you do that, Conall Weaver?"

"Oh, yes. I'm just flesh and blood. 'Cut me, do I not bleed?'"

The hatchet-faced king looked around him. A blade of sun slashed through the gap in the curtain and severed the room in two. The bed seemed to sag under his scrutiny. Everything seemed poorer and barer than before.

"It's very…plumb," he said, "a good chamber."

"I suppose so." Conall twisted a bit of paper between his fingers.

"No, I wouldn't kill my life if I slept in this fine place," Brennus told him. His words had the air of royal judgment.

"Don't you like the wattled huts of your people?"

"What does that have to do with whether you should kill your life or whether this is a pleasing chamber? There is a fine chair that swoops, too." A little of his usual sternness, even a touch of menace, had crept back into the king's voice. The chair jolted back and forth on the floorboards.

"You crafted me," the king said, "so that I could never live anywhere else but the Pictish hills because the wind in the heather would be calling my name, always and ever, until my heart broke from being away from the moors. The land is like me, and I am like it. I never asked to be made so dark and fierce, my blood circling like a hawk. Yet I am who I am, and my heartstrings are woven into the wattle of the people's huts. I'd rather live in the fens, where faces blink out at you and vanish, than live so far away from the Picts as this. It has the feel of another world. But there's nothing wrong with a little spying about, here or in Rome."

"Spy away," Conall said, tossing the corkscrew of paper to the floor.

"You don't like it here? Come to the hills with me. You can teach the men that chesting business that you do—"

"Boxing."

"Yes, the boxing."

Springs squawked as Conall moved from a straight chair to the bed.

"I don't hate Texas," he murmured, propping himself up on an arm. "Even if I am practically crucified in the dead center of Cross Plains. The sky is so big that it makes everything else small—a body is just a nubbin under a swath of blue."

"What happens to my people if you do this thing?"

"What thing?"

"The killing." Brennus spat onto the floor, and Conall stared at the glob of barbarian spittle.

"Nothing. You'd just go on the same way. Probably nothing much would happen."

"That wouldn't be so bad." The king wavered like a mirage. "The Picts could do with some tedium."

Even after Brennus broke apart and then disappeared entirely, Conall could hear his voice saying, "But it's fool work for a young man, killing his own life."

The Sickroom

"Could I revive within me / Her symphony and song…"

Conall's voice trailed away. Was his mother asleep and gone beyond all listening to poems? When he leaned forward and his shadow crossed her face, the eyes opened.

They seemed darker than before—wholly pupil now. The stare plucked at him. He felt the tug, just as if the claws of her hands snatched at his arm.

The bindings she had lain over him years ago seemed to respond with a faint humming vibration. He rubbed a hand across his face to clear away strange thoughts. Unbidden, an idea had drifted into his mind—that she had been the Abyssinian maid in Kubla Khan and that he had been the sweet infant dulcimer she played, tightening its strings, strumming a weird tune. Perhaps she was a witch. He met her eyes again. They demanded something from him. She couldn't speak. The acquired Irish lilt that made it clear she lived in another world than this was gone. Pneumonia had stolen her voice and now spoke in its own, a bubbling that could be heard through the cave of her ribs. He was too exhausted to answer what the eyes asked, but he sought her hand among the bedclothes all the same. The fingers had gathered together like a ghastly blossom with five petals of bone. Gradually they responded to his touch.

"Do you want something? Can I get you anything?"

He put the pencil in her hand. It took a long time for her to grasp the shaft and write a few waving letters on the school tablet.

"S-t-o-r. You want me to tell you a story?"

"Y" meant yes, or perhaps she was simply finishing the word.

He couldn't remember any of his own tales. Poe, Wildsmith, Shakespeare: the world's tales blew in the wind like a harvest of yellow leaves, but he couldn't catch one. All he could remember was the poem he had been reading, with its long introduction that told how the poet had fallen into a laudanum dream that swept him to Kubla Khan's palace. But a churlish fellow had come from Porlock and wakened him. The flowering trees with their candelabras of burning fragrance and the sacred river glittering its merriment in the sun or bursting from the tunnels of caves could not stand the touch of the person from Porlock. Probably he had brought something wholly unlovely—a side of mutton and an unpaid butcher's bill, say, or maybe a disapproving matron from Cross Plains. The lovely soap bubble fled, never to be recaptured.

Conall remembered the last time he had heard someone recite the poem, and how terribly sad and confusing it had been. They had been at one of the Caddo mountains, and everything had gone smash in the end. He did not want to think about that hour now or ever.

"Life's all somebody from Porlock," he said.

The wells of her eyes, glinting in rings of darkness, knew what he meant.

Because he could think of nothing else, he began to repeat the words of the poem that he had heard so many times—"In Xanadu did Kubla Khan / A stately pleasure-dome decree"—though he had already said the thing earlier and, besides, she knew the poem by heart. Surely the dream of a sacred river could go streaming through her mind whenever she liked.

When he finished saying the words, her hand slipped from his.

The eyes were on him again, plucking at him.

"It's going to be a hot day," he said. Picking up a damp rag, he wiped her mouth and laid the rag beside the bowl of water.

"I can't think of a story," he added. "They've all gone away, and I just can't write any new ones. Maybe I'm played out. Maybe I can come up with one later. My head's gone loggy."

She didn't look away but stared at him from those unblinking wells.

A fly bumbled in the corner of the window. He could feel that today was going to be one of those days when he could walk and walk under a blazing sun and never get to the horizon—and when he finally tottered from the edge into black oblivion, he would be awakened in the night. He would see the picture by his bed, his girl Maybelline with her head turned, smiling, a dimple shining out and something of the flash in the eyes showing the brightness of the light inside her. The thin material of a Sunday dress curved over her shoulder, the fabric so delicate and airy that she might have been wrapped in a petal. Then he would remember that Maybelline was going to leave, moving away to school in Baton Rouge, or realize that she was seeing somebody else, and he would feel like a damn crazy fool.

All their easy friendship had been changed to hurt. Only yesterday she had railed at him for romanticizing a gunman like Dillinger, when all he'd been saying was that he couldn't blame the fellow for shooting up a bank. Hadn't bank crashes stolen his own hard-earned cash, his hours of hammering yarns on the Underwood?

Soon he would be left companionless. Then he would be nothing but the village mockery in cap and bells, the one whose blood and sweat could never be praised as a man's work.

Sometimes he would get out of bed and type a letter to Wildsmith or some other storyteller. But they had turned into ghosts for him, wandering out there in the world where he could not go, and Conall had almost stopped writing them. The spider lines of connection had tattered, the neat labyrinth become a scribbled maze. But maybe he would write the editors who owed him money.

At some point he would hear what had roused him, the fluid struggling in his mother's throat, her dreadful throat-singing. A riptide of confused feeling would wash over him, dragging him to the bottom of a shadowy sea. He never tried to sort out what was most pressing in his mind, battered by a strange surf composed of resentment and love, horror and pity, along with an admiration for human endurance that goes on and on until in the end it becomes a kind of courage.

Now she made a noise as though she were drowning, and he got up again and rearranged the pillows under her back.

"That's better," he said, and sat down.

He might have dozed for a minute in the chair. He wasn't sure.

Sitting up straight, he looked around at the bed and chairs and dresser as though he had tumbled from his world into another. They seemed like something on the other side of sleep, plumped and soft like newly crammed feather pillows. On the bed, Maeve had dwindled to a stick figure next to their health and sleek abundance.

He was not at all surprised when an olive-skinned woman opened the door and entered. Her silky dress bore a pattern of brown and mauve orchids. She came to him and stood between his splayed-apart knees. Her hand was cool against his cheek.

"I am the goddess Melancholia," she told him.

Opening his arms, he embraced her, and she curled against him, pressing against his chest and wrapping her arms around his neck. Her bottom was wide and round, the breasts in her unbuttoned bodice like doves curled in sleep. She must have come straight from the kitchen because she smelled of molasses and burnt sugar, and for an instant his whole body responded to hers as with an electric current.

Then she began to sink into him, seeping through his pores into his flesh and bloodstream, flooding his lungs, winding through his veins toward the heart. He choked, gasping as he breathed her in.

"Ah!" He jumped up from the chair, fully awake.

His mother watched him from the bed, unmoving, her breath making a crackling sound from the half-open mouth.

"I was dreaming." He sat back down and rubbed at his temples. "I was really dreaming. But I dreamed that I was awake. Was that Aunt Lachesis Jones? She came into the room, only she was young. And darker than I remember."

Like a little white-haired monkey, Maeve stared at him intently.

"A story," he remembered. "You wanted a story."

Melancholia stirred inside him, looking out of his eyes at the poor monkey, and he knew that it had been only half a dream. The room returned to its former appearance. A smell of sickness and bitter medicine settled in the air, banishing any odor of burnt sugar.

Conall took the bowl and dirty rags away and fetched fresh water. When he came back, his mother's eyes were nearly closed, the lids rimmed with red.

He wondered if she could sleep propped up on the pillow, or if he should lower her. But her breath was bubbling so loudly that he felt a dread at the thought. What if she should drown, the fluid in her lungs welling up?

The lid over her left eye hung crinkled and askew. She was looking at him from under its crooked shade.

A story. She wants a story. All right. I can do this. I can.

"The *morin khuur* whinnied like a horse running free in the windswept Mongolian grasslands," Conall began, "and the young man played on its strings with a horsehair bow inside the emperor's *ger*, around a wood frame sheathed in felt and ornamented on the inside with sacred patterns. He wore a deep blue *del* tied with a sash, with loose trousers underneath, and he was a brave sight, handsome and tall, the fiddle held loosely between his legs.

"He sang to an ancient tune that he had heard an old woman hum when he was a small boy. The new words said that the fairer the scene, the more luxurious the bed and rugs, the finer the food, the more he felt the lack of his stolen bride. She was meant for him before the stars had been set alight, but now she was gone. A deep ache cut him in two, yet left him solitary. It no longer mattered that the cloth-of-gold tent shamed the sun or that a porcelain Chinese dragon chasing a pearl writhed in a place of honor or that he drank fresh mare's milk from a cup of Islamic glass. For without the girl who should have shared in these, all things had tumbled into shadow lands and become unreal, half transparent.

"The khan, having an empress and consorts, found the songs charming but free of any pang except a borrowed one. He paid well for the songs, and soon the musician tucked a bag of coins into his sash."

Conall stopped to listen. There was no sound but the bubbling from the lungs and the buzzing of the fly that bobbled against the panes, hunting for a way out. He swept a hand over his mother's eyes, and the lids closed.

"It's just as well," he said softly. "I don't have a story in me. Nothing was ever going to happen in that tale. Just more and more nothing."

He reflected that no hero could solve his current dilemmas and that no hero could fix the world. It was devilishly out of plumb and would never be straight.

"We need Mongolian windhorses around this place, to carry off the flies and whistle up some health and power," he told the room, half tongue-in-cheek, half serious. His sacrifice of the velvet bouquet at East Caddo—what were the mountains if not his holy places?—should have raised him a windhorse.

But perhaps it was impossible for him to regain his powers. A shaman would say that people who had an evil spirit were out of balance, ill, or bent toward their own destruction.

Maze of Blood

"I must be inhabited by a demon," he muttered.

If only that were the truth, it would explain so much! And all he would need to do was import a shaman from Mongolia to chase demons from his mother's lungs and from the corridors of veins that led to the innermost chambers of his heart where the red shadows lurked. Then the stories would come back, a little shy because they had been away, and the heroes who had gone off on distant journeys would come roistering home to Texas, demanding celebrations with new moonshine and apple stack cakes.

Vaquero

"That's dreadful! How can you?"

"How can I? Who else is there to do it? My father's always gone, or if he's home, he's sleeping. I've told you."

"How can he neglect his own wife when she's ill? And your work is as important as his or anybody else's—isn't that what you're always saying?"

"A doctor can't delay on a baby or a leg gone rotten with gangrene or a farm boy with a stiff neck and high fever."

"But Conall…"

Maybelline gave a little shiver, moving her shoulders uneasily, and her mouth drew into a moue of distaste.

Sometimes he had trouble reading her gestures and face, yet this time he knew exactly what she was saying. It had never occurred to him that what he was doing for his mother was in any way strange. He could feel the blood rushing to his cheeks and swung away to face the cool breeze on Mammy's front porch. His mother's flattened breasts, like two empty coin purses, floated into his mind. He thought of the puckered nipples, the bone cage of the ribs, the moss gone thin between her legs. He jerked his head to break the images and send them flying.

"Who else is there to do it?" He said the words again, testing the idea that there might be someone else—who?

"Your father's a doctor. Let him get some nurses if she needs changing in the night. You shouldn't be doing those intimate things for her."

He was silent.

"Conall, you know it's true. I don't understand how it is with your mother or why your father doesn't help more."

"She's not doing well. And being with her so much, I've lost the thread of my work."

Hens were making a sleepy fuss in a nearby chicken house, asking a question or two that gave rise not to answers but to more querulous noises.

"It'll come back again." Maybelline leaned against a porch pillar, her eyes straying to a lamplit window. "You're just worn out. Why don't you go away? You need to leave this town, to get away from all this sickness and see some new sights. Your father told me that you ought to go to England and Ireland. Why don't you?"

"A well can go dry," he said and, reminded of a poem by Coleridge, repeated the words softly:

Yet well I ken the banks where amaranths blow,
Have traced the fount whence streams of nectar flow,
Bloom, O ye amaranths! Bloom for whom ye may,
For me ye bloom not! Glide, rich streams, away!
With lips unbrightened, wreathless brow, I stroll:
And would you learn the spells that drowse my soul?
Work without Hope draws nectar in a sieve,
And Hope without an object cannot live.

"That's beautiful," she said, "but everything will be better when you are not so tired out by overwork. Then you'll begin to write."

For an instant, he thought Maybelline meant to embrace him, but then her voice changed and grew teasing. "Maybe you just need to shave off that horrible mustache, Conall. Did you ever think of that?"

He stared into the sea of blue twilight. Some rosiness from the sunset still lingered, tinting the horizon. How could she joke about a mustache? Didn't she realize that the slow drops of grief were welling magically from the deepest core of him and staining the very sky? What he wanted was for Maybelline to stretch out her hand and show love lying like a snowy trinket on her palm—to yield the alabaster heart to him without a sound. But it was possible that they had had too much of words, and talked their time quite away.

"Someday," he said, "I'll ride a horse across the taiga, and follow where the Mongols wreaked havoc across the world, the long way to China and the Sea of Japan. Or I'll gallop on the heels of Alexander the Great and visit the ruins that he left behind. That's what I'll do."

When he made those promises, Conall nearly believed them—was almost sure he would cross the ocean, see the Old World, and venture to the fabulous East. But as soon as the words stopped, he no longer had any faith. Melancholy rolled through his veins and settled, staking its claim on his heart. He would never go anywhere. In the end, he would die of weariness and be dropped into a Texas grave, and the rattlers would coil in the grass above and, given time, make their burrows in his cage of bones.

"Sure you will," she said softly. "That would be wonderful."

What was the use, he wondered, if Maybelline would not go with him? Who would lie with him in the long grass while the horse drank from a stream if not his girl? Did she see him now the way the others did? Once when he was small, a teacher told his mother that there was something off-kilter about his lunging walk, his too-big vocabulary, and his penchant for hiding in corners with a book.

"Most of the time, he doesn't even pay attention," she had complained. "He looks over my shoulder, or out the window, as if he sees another world."

"Perhaps he does," Maeve said.

His mother had worn a hat with a veil to the meeting, and both her refinement and her Irish accent grew stronger as the conversation went on. She never lifted the veil.

Always, he was different. Always.

He had been prisoned in a labyrinth at birth, and never found a way out. Lately it seemed that he had a chance. Doors to the outside had come ajar. He caught a glimpse of Providence in his letters to Wildsmith—the lost family house on Angell Street, the pencils of sculls at a distance on the river, and ghostly figures teetering arm in arm on the winding paths of Swan Point Cemetery. He could picture those scenes, imagine that one day he would walk those streets, wander the paths through an ornate graveyard. Other doors swung open like the windows of the German Christmas calendar that had hung inside the door of his sixth-grade classroom. Each day, a child was allowed to open a different window until they reached Christmas Day. On the final day of school before Christmas, he had been permitted to finish opening the last week of windows while the others watched. Letters from editors and other writers had been like those childhood windows, bits of paper folding back to reveal new landscapes.

And then there was Maybelline.

Once he felt sure that she would be the one to transform his world for good. If only he had acted before the shadows started to fall between them. But he hadn't been free then, and he wasn't now.

Like honey in a glass tilted to one side and then the other, melancholy moved heavily in him. No matter what he did, he couldn't evade its presence. For some months past, he had thought that Maybelline would drive melancholy away from him. Now he knew that its thick substance had stopped his mouth when he should have spoken.

"I'm nothing but a hack," he said, "a no-account failure. I should have been a professional boxer, not a writer."

"You don't mean that," she said. "I know you don't mean it. I am certain it's hard being a writer. I've felt it so. There's a lot of disappointment and grief, even if you're a success—and you are. People write you letters from all over the world."

The words held no comfort for him. How could they? He had never fit in anywhere and never would, though for a time he had dreamed it could be otherwise. That was the truth that mattered in his life.

The little Coleridge poem, "Reality's Dark Dream," streamed through his head, with its final questions: "Must I die under it? Is no one near? / Will no one hear these stifled groans and wake me?"

He soon left, feeling even more the fool, knowing that she would be seeing Fletcher in the evening. She was not his girl, not anymore.

In the next weeks he didn't see Maybelline.

He wrote a fragment of a story.

Several times he took his mother to see out-of-town doctors, but he ended by thinking that old Doc was better at keeping her alive than these younger, fresher doctors with the crisp diplomas.

Still, he kept taking her to see them in hopes of better, more pleasing verdicts. One afternoon while she was being examined, he wandered down an unfamiliar street, and a window display of piled sombreros and ten-gallon hats caught his eye. He walked into the shop, the brass bell jangling. Mountains of hats, bandanas, boots, and pants rose from the counters and central table.

Conall reached for a bright red bandana.

He plucked up a black sombrero. Dangling pompom balls trembled as he turned his head.

He chose a pair of black pants, cut a little short.

Outside in the Texas glare, he roared with laughter. A young girl looked up at him and scuttled away. He wiped his eyes on the back of his hand and thought, *So this is why I've been growing a mustache!* Tying the bandanna around his neck, he plunked the sombrero on his head and fastened the chin strap.

"Vaquero!" He laughed again.

On reaching the office, he talked briefly with the doctor, who gave him a handwritten list of instructions and told him to bring his mother back in a month. The man seemed distracted by Conall's sombrero, and his eyes kept moving to the pompoms dancing cheerfully below the brim.

Maeve was dozing in the waiting room, a packet of medicine in her lap. The shadow of the hat slid over her face.

She woke, looked up at him, and blinked.

He didn't mention the get-up—just swooped the hat from his head and bowed, offering her the support of his arm.

Tossing the black pants onto the car seat, Conall steered his mother inside and went around to the driver's side, whistling. She stared at him. She looked exactly the same as before, but he had changed.

If people wanted to think that a writer was a damn freak and a fool, so be it!

He would wear his Texas fool's cap and bells, and he would shake them in their faces. With his sombrero and bandanna, he would defy them all, every one—even his mother and father and Maybelline and his friends. If they would not acknowledge him, he would force them to do so. If they wanted him ostracized and alone, he would show them just how proud and unsociable he could be. He would flaunt his black and red costume in each and every godforsaken face.

For once he felt bigger than life.

With this disguise he might even escape that bitch, Melancholia.

Conall pressed on the accelerator, and the car leaped down the straight Texas highway as if fleeing from that nectar-lipped goddess. His mother slumped against the door, her unkempt hair ruffled by the wind. One of Doc's sayings sprang into mind. *Fine as frog's hair.* Giving a maniacal laugh that set the little balls on the hat to jiggling, he swept down the road.

The Flying Horse

Sure enough, Conall the Vaquero became the ten days' wonder of the town. He was hooted at and mocked, and once two little boys swaggered behind him in imitation, holding their hands far apart to indicate the wideness of their invisible hats. When she encountered him outside the post office, Maybelline fled, her heels rat-a-tat-tatting on the boards laid across the road.

Under the pressure of losing her forever, he put on the suit and fedora that she liked and went to call. His mother was dying, he said. A terrible freedom yawned ahead of him. He told Maybelline plainly that he needed a woman to share his life and to love him. What could have been more desperate and direct than that? But they were past the days when he had felt certain that she cared about him. Long ago, he should have shouted to her, *I need to give my life to you. I love you. Will you marry me?* Hat in hand, he was now driven to begging, telling her that he possessed nothing—all his words having burned to ash without, phoenix-like, suffering a new birth. Nor did he have her love to make life bearable.

That afternoon sailed into the past, and she was gone.

On the verge of leaving, she had been merry, flitting from topic to topic and making jokes. She told him that he ought to take a razor to his walrus mustache, for with a clean-scraped face he would certainly find true love. Slippery with excitement over the move to Baton Rouge and graduate school, she could not be pinned down. She would write. Of course, she would write him. And she would be back to the farm for visits. She would miss the bullbats sailing overhead while songbirds sleepily chirped in their nests and Mammy chased the cows in for the night. A thousand things would be calling her name—the rosy fruits of the pincushion cacti, the mockingbirds and whippoorwills, the fervor of a Texas sunset, and the storms spreading like a stain on damp paper.

Afterward, his father brought home the history Conall meant Maybelline to keep as a parting gift. She had dropped it at Doc's office on her way out of town. A thick block of the world's ages, the book now lay by the Underwood. Strange how much its return bothered the giver…like a final slap in the face, though perhaps she hadn't meant it so.

No letter came.

She would be settling into her room and taking her theater courses by genuine Texas storm, he had no doubt. But she had not thought of him, at least not enough to send so much as a postcard's *All well, wish you were here—M.* Caught up in her new world, Maybelline must have forgotten him.

Letters from others arrived. Unread, they collected in a stack on the history book and eventually spilled onto the floor.

Whenever he managed to catch some sleep, Conall woke feeling worse than before. When he nodded off, Melancholia followed him to bed and pursued him in dreams. His sheets were imbued with the odor of burnt cane and molasses. She moved in him like a sand dune trapped in an enormous hourglass.

Suspends what nature gave me at my birth. The line trickled through his head like a drop of liquid fire. It was Coleridge again, with "Dejection: An Ode." How often his mother had read the poem to him, as if to make him what he had become—poet, storyteller, melancholic.

The newly hired nurses wouldn't let him rest. Every time he went to lie down, there was some question, or else they came to his bedroom and whispered that Maeve wanted him, and was he awake?

But he would be better soon. When he grasped his freedom and left Cross Plains, he would see the crown that was Stonehenge rising from mist. He would sail to the green hills of Ireland and hear the streams caroling through ancient peat cuttings. In Mongolia, a shaman would clamber up the world tree and heal him, setting his feet where they should stand.

Conall drank so much coffee that his hands became tremulous. Bottle flies seemed to be burrowing into his brain, planting seeds of unpleasant buzz. Most of his days and nights were spent beside his mother's bed. Sometimes he dozed in a chair, sometimes he woke to find her sleeping or watching him—little else was left for her to do except to listen as he read from her favorite poems. As her life dwindled, the labor of caring for her seemed to swell until the house was jammed with helpers.

Maeve's breath moved in and out more quickly, and once she hemorrhaged onto the bedclothes. She knew Conall less often now—and he was the only one. She stared at the others without recognition.

Melancholia walked with him, strewing the dead leaves of tales and trees before him. When he could not go on, she groped inside him. She shaded the Texas sun from his face. She kissed him full on the lips.

His mind bumbled from reality to dream, dream to reality. Sometimes it stayed, snared halfway in between, for many minutes. When that happened, he drank more coffee and sat up straighter until the next time. His stomach ached from the drink and the aspirin he downed in the faint hope of feeling better. His skull seemed to pound in time with the beat of his heart.

One morning before the dawn, he dreamed up a story.

A funeral escort of cowboys on horseback was ambling behind a Conestoga wagon, the horses easing through the long prairie grass. The men joshed and told tall tales, and they killed everything alive that they passed—rattlesnakes, prairie dogs, armadillos, coyotes, wolves, tigers, and the burning leopards of the sun. Inside the wagon lay a dead boy and a dead dog, and driving the oxen and cracking the whip was the boy's own mother.

After days of travel, they reached a blood-red tomb in a green wilderness of larches and willows. The cowboys buried the boy and dog, and covered the place with dirt. Afterward, they drove mustangs over the ground until the site was obliterated and looked like bare dirt after a big cattle drive. Bringing mesquite trees and cacti, the cowboys planted the soil, cussing a blue streak all the while. They galloped to the sea and filled their boots and saddlebags with sand before riding hard to the grave and pouring it out again. With small combs of Bakelite and wood, they raked the sands into ripples. When they were done, the tallest cowboy took a rope and lassoed a river to divert its course. Under earth and dune and current, the boy and dog went on sleeping, while the mother sat on a stone in the stream with her chin in her hand.

Conell tilted his neck to one side, then another, hearing the bones rub and crack together. A story like that one was no damn good to sell.

His mother would never be sitting on a stone again. She lay stretched on the rack of the bed in the interminable days of her long dying.

While he was dreaming up a cowboy cortege, Mrs. Thorncroft had come into the room and was moving like a shadow on the far side of the bed. Her feet were soundless on the floor. She must have slipped off her shoes, fearing to wake him, but Conall was awake, staring into the dark. He listened as she poured water into a basin and, in a few moments, wrung out a cloth.

The sky began to lighten.

Mrs. Thorncroft tugged a pad into place under his mother's hips and changed the dirty gown, and then left the room with a sack of fouled linen. She spoke to the men in the living room. Dr. Edenfield and his father came in and were unable to rouse Maeve, though this was no surprise. She had been in a stupor since about noon the previous day.

The arm was limp when Dr. Edenfield checked her pulse. Her breathing had altered again, becoming even more rapid and shallow, and she was now running a fever.

Her body reminded Conall of a flung rag doll. Bending, their backs to him, the two doctors arranged her limbs in a more natural-looking position.

"No response to sound. No response to touch." Dr. Edenfield nodded to his colleague. Taking a sharp pair of tweezers from his bag, he pinched her finger.

Nothing.

"Nor to pain. Did you see the pupils?"

"Yes." Doc straightened and exchanged a glance with Dr. Edenfield before turning to his son.

"Don't you want to get some sleep?" Doc Weaver's hand brushed against his son's arm.

"No thanks," Conall said, "not yet."

The setting moon appeared in the corner of a windowpane. He got up from the chair and raised the sash, propping it on a stick. His skin prickled at the touch of coolness. The wind, which had been tossing some bits of velvet petals on Caddo Peak East only minutes before, spiraled through the house, caressing the dying woman's face and rearranging her hair.

The neighbor ladies who had come by to cook breakfast for the doctors could now be heard chatting in the side yard. The thought of food made Conall nauseous. Dr. Edenfield brought him another cup of coffee and returned to the kitchen, where he and Doc would be sitting down at the table to eat a generous breakfast of biscuits with preserves, hash made with beef and gravy and onions, grits, and fried eggs. The spurt of water from the pump out back meant that Mrs. Thorncroft was putting the pad to soak in a pail with some Duz soap and rinsing the gown.

Reality's dark dream.

Was it the sound of the water or the imagined words that startled Conall? He was so weary that he had begun to dream while awake.

Dry grains slipped through the neck of the hourglass and sprinkled onto the sand dune below.

The substance of time alternately crumpled and was pulled taut, like a bolt of silk in a clerk's hands, counted out yard by yard against a measuring stick.

He could hear the clock on the other side of the room. It reminded him of the bird that used to peck against the glass.

Peck, peck, peck...

Maybelline flew in the window in the shape of a tiny, tiny cardinal and sat on his knee. He spoke to her with his mind.

Did you know that the lady cardinal is one of the few North American female songbirds that likes to sing, and that she and her mate share some of the same song lines? Did you know that she sings when she sits on her nest? Did you know that he is wilder in color than she is, and that she calls to him when she sings? That she predicts the rain? That she is the daughter of the sun?

The little cardinal shifted her weight and looked at him.

Of course you did. Because you're a cardinal. How could you not? You own the star of the sun and you sing for the rain.

"I know what it is now," he told her.

She tilted her head, eyes so dark brown they looked like jet.

"Love is like a bird. That's why the old Greek writers gave Eros a pair of wings. You can catch the little flying creature in your hand and keep it, and your fingers will be the bars that curl into a cage. Then it will stay in the dark, its glory never seen or known."

Her feet tickled his knee through the coarse pants.

"If you let the thing loose, it will fly away toward the dawn, singing."

And it will never come back, Conall thought.

The bird twitched its wings and was gone. Outside, the other birds were awakening under the gaudy immensity of sunrise. A mockingbird caroled the news of morning to every blessed rooster along Turkey Creek.

He could hear a clatter of silver from the kitchen, where Mrs. Thorncroft and the doctors were talking in low voices. When she returned to the dying woman's chamber, the nurse barely touched him on the shoulder with her palm. Conall heard his own voice ask if his mother would ever return to wakefulness.

"No, dear," she said, "not from a coma like this one. You needn't stay. You've done every bit you can do. Get some rest now. It's nearly over. She might last another day, but she won't never know you."

Outside, the air against his skin made him shudder. Reflux brought the taste of bile to his mouth, and he spat. His throat burned. Reeling, he seized the pillar of the porch with both hands, and his eyes crawled slowly over the swing and the pale ceiling that his mother had said kept the dirt daubers away because they didn't like blue. A cardinal split the yard in half, shrieking words he couldn't understand. The whine of insects needled past the ringing in his ears.

When he heard Mrs. Thorncroft repeat her words—*nearly over, won't never know you*—he looked around, but she was nowhere to be seen.

Just a dream, he said to himself, or perhaps aloud.

He wrenched open the car door, sat, and then jerked at the handle to the glove box. The Colt .38 gleamed inside. Since the gun was not his, he had been careful to oil it. The model had a satisfying bang, and no recoil to speak of, and the trip up Caddo Peak East had proved that it handled well. A silver colt bucked on the diamond-patterned grip. A chill born of sleeplessness and anticipation flashed over him. In a single burst of something like prayer, he yielded to whatever lay beyond.

Fly, little horse.

Racking the slide, he chambered a round. He placed the mouth of the gun against his skull and fired.

Tree

It was the eighth hour.

He slowed down, walking away from the blood-red labyrinth. Behind him the walls made a puzzle that spilled across a low hillock. He kept moving. The world tree stretched above him, nailed to the sky by a star in the shape of Texas. The figure pinned to the tree by cactus spines was sometimes one thing, sometimes another—old Yahweh or mother or dove or a snake-man who had twined three times around the bole.

A horned preacher on a soapbox damned his carcass to hell, pointing towards the roots that arched and knotted and dived, puncturing the ground.

Later on, a girl brought him a drink, carrying it in a cup made from a furled leaf. Behind him, some of the spilled water tried to take the shape of a small dog and run at his heels. After falling back into a puddle, the water sprouted wings and flew away.

His jumbled lives—dreams, perhaps—jostled and laughed and cried out for more, but now he stumbled into shadows.

A low bellowing filled the air.

When the echoes died away, he could no longer summon words. The red maze and the tree rippled and broke apart into small black letters.

The rest was a blank page.

Metamorphosis

Inside his cocoon of sheets, something was happening to Conall. Elsewhere, the word flashed round Cross Plains like prairie fire, wind-whipped.

Conall Weaver hammered out a poem on his Underwood before he went for the gun.

Hellbound, Conall dropped like starry Lucifer from the ramparts of his world, sliding like a tear along the cheek of night.

Conall Weaver was a dadgum cotton-picking loony who couldn't tell the difference between a story and real life.

Arms straining at the air, Conall Weaver wrestled with God.

Conall Weaver had the Oedipus complex.

Conall Weaver roared into the desert, where he stared at the rose window of the sun until it exploded into a kaleidoscope of glass.

Hush! Pray now, you Southern children, all you sweet sinners! Conall Weaver, Conall Weaver, he wasn't made for your judgings.

Conall was breathing still, but now between one breath and another he was becoming a Texas tall tale. Hadn't he stretched one often enough? This tale he had never told, but it would sure-fire sell. The story settled around him like a too-big shroud, puffed by his final gasps.

He would grow into it.

After his next breath, Conall Weaver would be fiction.

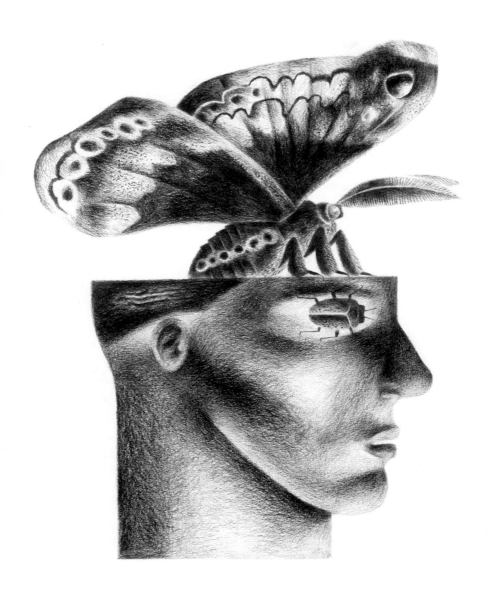

Man in the Maze

The Emperor's Grave

In other lives Conall was a minor warrior and bard.

So he had often claimed, and the boast served him as the truth because his only freedom was to tell tales and sink deeply into what he called *memories*. The idea appeased some deep-rooted rage for order—for bringing his ragtag life closer to the shapeliness and substance of his daydreams.

In time he came to spend more time in these dreams than in what his townspeople called *the real world*.

"The fabulous burial of the khan" was a story of another Conall who lived in another time and place. His name was *Tolui*, the same as the khan's youngest son. Tolui had been what Conall desired to be in the maze of his innermost self—a battler, a rover, and a shaper of words. His ties were not to women but to fellow warriors and to his liege lord, a ruler so charismatic and powerful that he was hailed as the King of Kings.

At the death of Genghis Khan, Tolui rode with the funeral cortege, the great river of men flooding the plains as they surrounded the body of their leader, driving toward Khentii Aimag where the khan had been born with a clot grasped in his fist so that everyone in the clan knew he had a destiny of blood.

The future ruler was named *Temujin* after a Tatar chieftain captured by his father.

The Fabulous Burial of the Khan

Tolui had been a warrior once, but he had taken three arrows in the hip and now walked with a limp and was good for nothing in the way of fighting. Nevertheless, a lifetime of much Mongol meat and milk had made him strong, and he could stand a day's ride on his bay horse and still tell tales about Temujin when they camped for the night.

Genghis would have an unmarked, secret grave. His first wish had been to rule his enemies and the world, and that he had done, or close enough, conquering lands and seeding the wombs of women. His second wish was to escape death, but when it became clear that neither shaman nor monk could help him do so, he asked for a hidden resting place.

In death as in life, his passage meant danger. When the escort passed an old man with a wooden staff, an *arban* of men broke away and killed him where he stood, even though he was blind. Polished by many years of caressing, the staff gleamed under his dead hand. A little girl playing with twigs was chased three or four feet before her head sailed up like a silk ball. A young woman bathing in the stream, her hair lying close on her spine, a lustrous black wing…what happened to her could bring on more tears than a sea can hold. Though one of the many thousands of the khan's children, she remained the only one whose destiny was tied to the dead man's escort. Whole families were slaughtered because a ger hunched like a stone in the path of the flood that carried the khan—posthumously to be named *emperor*—to his grave. Unlike most rulers, he was even larger and more fearsome in death than in life. Whether dog, marmot, or red deer, whatever stepped into the flesh-and-bone torrent of his warriors died.

In the evenings, Tolui sang in his throat to soothe comrades in the cortege or else told stories to praise the khan and the martial exploits of the past. He began with the boyhood of Genghis Khan. When he was six, Temujin had wandered away from his family and ended up in the high rocks and ice of the mountains, and there he killed a shadowy snow leopard with a single arrow. Home again, he became the man of the family at nine after his father, the clan leader, was poisoned. Cast out by the clan, Temujin and his close kin survived, and his mother taught him all that he needed to learn in order to become khan. With another arrow, he slew a half-brother for stealing food. He tightened his sash, endured the starving time, and married. At sixteen he forged alliances and raided the Merkit tribe to rescue his stolen bride.

With words and wild gestures by the fire, Tolui reminded the men of Mongol power.

"Dynasty after dynasty fell to our khan. We scythed the armies, sowed the hillsides with their bones! Their captured rulers were given noble 'bloodless deaths,' pressed under caskets of their own jewels, given molten gold to drink, suffocated with feathers, or broken with iron bars. The cities became Mongol or else were plundered. Sweet were those days of pillage, when the pale thighs of virgins were streaked with blood!"

At the end of the journey, when the khan's body was secreted in the earth, it was Tolui who devised the tall tales that the few surviving soldiers would tell.

"Our khan admired artisans," he said. "Often he would spare the life of someone who could weave with gold thread or who had learned to illuminate books. Make what you tell others about his grave into a heavenly gift to the khan. That story is not a lie. It stands for the mysteriousness and secrecy of his tomb."

"Like this," he told them, holding out his arms as if in supplication. "Ask, 'Who knows where the emperor's bones lie dreaming?' Answer, 'The Mongol Empire goes on, as if forever, from the Caspian to the Sea of Japan. Somewhere in all this distance of taiga and desert, field and mountain, three *tumen*—thirty thousand soldiers—scoured a new course for the Onon River. Set free in its new course, the thrust of pent-up water tossed a score of them into the air as it buried the emperor.'"

Another version of this fabulation claimed that a flood from heaven had gouged a hole in the earth for the grave, paused for the burial, and then left behind a lake where a bowl of grass had once lain. Yet a third version said that his body had been tucked among the roots of the world tree and that his suns-soul now paddled a cloud among the sky spirits, bringing rain and fertility to the Mongol people.

"Tell them that the body of the khan was planted deep into the soil," Tolui said. "Tell them that afterward our horses stampeded back and forth through a remote valley until every sharp blade of meadow grass and every soft flower vanished and no one could tell where the grave lay. The soldiers then dug tall trees, carried them horizontally as one carries a siege engine, and nestled their roots tenderly inside pits in the ground. A party of men was left to water the new forest for a year and day."

Another of Tolui's tales asserted that a desert covered the emperor. Loons and goldeneye ducks brought the desert, grain by grain, and made it round like a ger. Then the winds came and made the place their prey, blowing the sand into unreadable shapes of mystery.

"To this very hour, the resting place of Genghis Khan has not been found," Conall said aloud, sitting in front of his Underwood, "and not one of us who still lives and remembers will ever tell."

Sometimes his friends from school marveled because he seemed so lightly tethered to reality, the edges of their world and other worlds blurring under his fingers. It seemed that he hated the little Texas town, and often he said that its bustle spoke to him of mendacity and greed lingering like a shadow from the boomtown days. He often

Maze of Blood

talked about death, his own or of some famous man from the past—
even his prior deaths, which he claimed to have suffered long ago in
the destruction of Atlantis or in the red battlefields and elegant courts
of Asia and Europe.

No one could make him hold fast to a hope for a long life of
stories and books and family. No one could make him believe that
the future of a young man called *Conall Weaver* was worth the living.

Maybelline

The girl broke into his house like a wave.

Windows were thrown open to let the breeze in, and the crickets sawed like mad on their dry, chitinous fiddles. Somewhere in the background a radio played a cowboy song about horse thieves and a broken heart. Conall had been rattling the Underwood's keys and ranting a story to the air when she sailed through the door and splashed against the walls.

His mother and father tried to turn her away, as if pushing with their dried, withered fingers against the blue-and-green swell of a mermaid. But her voice rang out so loudly that she woke him from a tale of bushwhacking across the wilderness, and he came into the living room.

Her brown eyes held his.

He could feel the walls starting to buckle—could feel some kind of radiance pouring out of her and pushing at the meager room, making the dilapidated couch and chairs stand out in all their cheerlessness. Perfume blossomed in the air that had been stale and smelled faintly of illness. Her presence diminished his mother and father, and they dwindled to toys. She might as well have been a tiger roaming the Sikhote-Alin mountains, and they two little rabbits in the ginseng leaves! Her body moved easily, as if she were more at home in the house than they, with more of a right to be there. Conall felt a ripple of pleasure—or gratefulness—perhaps even joy. Whatever it was, the sensation was so unfamiliar that he could not put a final name to it and knew only that for all his bulk, he felt very light on feet that seemed about to float up from the floor. He wanted to rush to her, wrap his arms around her, and sniff the scent of her hair, and he would have been content to hold her that way for a long time.

"You reminded me of a poem," he told her, later on in the evening.

"What poem?"

"'Kubla Khan.' The way the water goes dancing and diving."

"Next time I'll bring my dulcimer," she said.

"My Abyssinian maid," he said, and smiled.

"The Abyssinian maid melted away like the poem."

"I'll have to hold on tight," he said.

She dazzled him. A kind of bewitchment was shed from her fingertips as she spoke. In the distance, crickets were chirping, and a few spotted chorus frogs were throat-singing—their vocal sacs emitting a series of rasping trills. Conall said that the frogs had been Mongolians in another life but had been exiled to Texas to repent of their sins. He told her that he had called up the moon especially for her and that the harvest moon belonged to Ceres. Soon, he said, the daughter of the goddess would be leaving for the winter kingdom of Hades. He wondered how Persephone, so full of light and life, could endure such a kingdom of darkness.

Clinging close to the horizon, the enormous autumn moon had taken on the surprising color of a rutabaga. Perhaps they had danced under the moon together. Conall didn't know how to dance but couldn't imagine that ignorance would have stopped him. He could not remember, though he could still feel her hand that was small and warm and sweet-smelling. Perhaps the dancing had come later in his dreams.

Her name was *Maybelline*.

May bells.

He thought of Texas yellow bells, the wild blossom that was also called *esperanza* and *trumpet flower*.

Esperanza. Didn't that word translate into hope? And a yellow bells plant was strong as well as sweet. Not like him. What was he but some wild Texas grass—tumble or mesquite grass or red grama.

She wanted to be a writer—had already written stories. She kept journals, she said, for practice, and though he didn't see the least sense in writing down the ordinary minutiae of life, he was willing to think that it was fine.

"You'll write all this down, and you'll say how we met and what we said?" He wasn't sure he liked the idea. Surely he would appear as an idiot in the pages of her journal.

"Yes, all of it. Good practice for writing dialogue." When she smiled, a dimple appeared.

"Well, I don't know. You don't want people in stories to jaw just like they do in real life. A story's not real life. It would be powerfully boring to have your characters natter the way people go on and on about things that don't amount to a hill of beans. Take some little piece of nothing-news or weather or scrap-of-bad-health, and drag it by the hair for a few dozen miles, until the other person listening feels stomped by mules and is glad to see some other poor miserable fool come along and relieve them of the burden of carrying on what passes for a conversation. Dialogue in a tale is like sleight-of-hand with a magician. The usual words are stirred about differently. A lot is left out, and the magic of the thing catches you. That's what I think."

She didn't mind a little disagreement. She would write his advice down and consider it, and she was willing to be convinced.

In the yard he held her hand, there in the moonlight, and stood close to her, drinking in the perfume and the faint odor of soap and lotion.

"Maybelline," he said, "you're rarer than a bluebird from a blue moon. You're as precious as pay dirt. I believe that you must have flown in from Venus. Maybe from the tiptop of the world tree, from where the North Star is glittering. A girl that cares about what I care about—I've never met one before."

"The world tree," she repeated.

"That's—I'll tell you about it some day. I'll tell you about Mongolia and Genghis Khan. That's a powerful story, and it's real. Realer than people talking about the fluctuating price of cotton in front of Higgenbotham's General Store or chatting about the curd in Aunt Florrie Mae's lemon meringue pie, and wondering how she manages to keep those little bitty globules of amber from beading up on top."

Maybelline had come to meet him because she wanted to talk about writing, but there were things she knew that Conall didn't grasp. He could tell because of the way she had breezed into the house that she had something he didn't. He admired her. She hadn't been stopped by his father, so querulous and protective, or by his mother's naked attempt to reproach him for leaving the house. "Run along and forget me if you can," Maeve had said in her weak invalid's voice. At those words, the girl seemed to glow higher than ever, like a fire showered with splinters of pine fatwood.

She had a golden aura about her, invisible to the eye but detectible to Conall's senses. He imagined with pleasure that she might be one of the elemental creatures he had read about in books of mythologies, the spirit of a zephyr or a star or a tidal current. Maybe she was all those things, wave and wind and fire—the lithe spirit of a river made out of windblown sparks and yellow bells! It was astonishing how easily she had burst open the doors and swept him from the living room.

Hadn't she asked him questions about his writing, and hadn't he answered? He laughed, his voice soft and low. What a hoot! What a damn crazy thing, that he couldn't remember much of anything at all except the joyful oceanic wave crashing into the room and the rutabaga moon and the smell of her hair. He must have been in some kind of altered consciousness!

She had talked about how folks thought she was wasting her time when she wrote stories. He recalled that part of the evening because it was such a familiar tune. Somebody had told her that she should get a job at the five-and-dime store, that a friend who worked there earned nine dollars a week.

He groaned, his fingers curling into fists as though he could batter some sense into Cross Plains. These damn people wanted a girl like a river spirit who streamed with golden fire to sell her soul for nine dollars a week! Why, it was like cutting down a live oak in order to mill some toothpicks. But that's how it was in this godforsaken podunk county. *The Sahara of the Bozart*, that's what Mencken had called the South.

Conall had started to fume about two-bit burgs that didn't know anything about art or stories and didn't care about beauty because all they wanted was money. But when Maybelline took him by the hand, he forgot all about the soul-eaters of small-town Texas and shut his mouth. The golden light in her fingers had bathed his own until he could think of nothing but staying close to its warmth.

He could recall only a couple of things in his life that had made him feel so careless and alive and happy. One was the dog, Caradog, who all his days had asked for nothing but to leap with him in the sun or to lie close to him on the bed at night but now lay rotting in an unmarked grave somewhere in the back lot. The other was the day he had sold his first story to *Weird Tales*. His relief and gladness ran so deep that he had knelt by the bed and prayed to Yahweh and the Son and the Holy Spirit, right in front of Fletcher!

Oh, he would kneel down again in thanks for this little bird, flown in through the open window. Old Noah didn't know the half of it, how glad a man could be to see a sweet feathered dove nestling in his hand. He would be willing to climb a thousand temple steps on his knees, just to clasp her in his arms.

Soon he would see her again. He had asked, and she agreed to see him the next night. There were things she wanted to know. It was amazing that she had found him in this wretched tumbleweed town caught in the claws of the Depression, that they had found each other despite the locals who thought he should be doing any kind of labor except the kind he was doing. These run-of-the-mill Texans couldn't see writing as work to be done or as a job, though he made more money than most of them. They couldn't see it as a calling.

But he thought that Maybelline could.

Ball of Fire

"I like to walk in the rain."

Such a simple liking for Maybelline to admit, but he loved the idea. Was there any other girl in all Texas who would say such a thing? He had seen women scuttling across the main street, sheets of newspapers held over their heads so that their crimped hair would not be mussed. Her hair always lay in neat waves, and yet she would walk in the rain. She didn't care about the bush-league rules of life the way the others cared.

And another thing: the Texas summer had turned to fall and fall to winter, and she still surprised him. Most people never surprised him or else were all used up in that way within a few days. But this girl, lithe and small, seemed packed with an infinite capacity to delight him with her thoughts.

She was his girl now, his best girl, his only girl, the one for whom he had been waiting for long millennia.

Each had joked about getting married but never on the same day. On a spring or summer afternoon, perhaps they would be of one mind, and then he would buy her a diamond ring like the ones they had looked at in the window of an out-of-town jeweler's.

When he was with her, he often forgot about his mother's claim on him, staked by the time he was five or six years old. Even so far back, he had promised to take care of Maeve forever. The tubercular woman had bound him with stories. For hours each day, she had turned her attention to reading tales and poems and laying down sediment of love and loyalty, fear and guilt that under great pressure metamorphosed to stone. Mother and son were different from others, singular and above the herd—above Doc, who liked to josh and yammer and glad-hand the world. They were alone with words under the immense Texas sky. By the time the Irish lilt first floated into Maeve's mouth, the two already lived in another universe. Faith, it was a better one than a realm of boomtowns and money-grubbers.

With Maybelline he didn't think about either his mother or his father for hours at a time, and when he did, he also remembered that a future would come when he would be free. They drove the back roads of Texas or poked around a far-off bookstore or walked under the moonlight, talking about stories and history and the nature of the world. The living room, the dying room, the place where Maeve sat, slowly sinking into the cushions, was as far away as Mongolia. It seemed almost as though he had grown up and moved away, steering his own free-roving life without a word from his mother.

Then he would remember her claim on him. Was it time for her medicine? Was that touch of pleurisy still hanging on? Would she be fagged out and wanting help to climb into bed? Had she had trouble breathing that morning, and would she be waiting, waiting for his return because Doc had gone out hours before and not come back?

A restlessness accompanied such thoughts. "I'd like to be a painted pinto pony," he once told Maybelline. "I'd like to crash all these walls and corridors that hem me in and to race the wind until I fly off the edge of the world."

When he kissed his only girl, he tasted a liberty that made him feel drunk, though he didn't say so. It made him want to kiss her again and again, but something held him back. What he frequently said was his old stand-by, "A woman ties a man down." Mostly, he meant it as a joke, but there was a hard, bitter kernel to the words that he did not see.

One afternoon he picked her up for a drive in the country. He liked it on the open road, where he would meet nobody from town and was never reminded that the people there saw him as a damn freak, and that for a citizen of Texas to spot a writer was as downright unnatural as one of them coming upon a fairy perched on a dilapidated picket fence in front of the old homestead. Chances are, that fey creature wouldn't have a chance. *Splat!* Down would flap the kitchen fly swat. And the fairy would be fresh trash for the burn barrel out back.

Yet the world was full of things just as peculiar—didn't birds sometimes nest in a cactus? That's what he was, a motley-colored bird who dipped and soared above the plain, meager world of his townspeople, and hid himself deep in a prickly cactus.

A wind from the north had begun to blow, and the temperature dropped steadily. Not five miles out of town, he noticed that the sky looked bruised. Most people stayed indoors when deep blue began to spread like ink in water, but he liked being out when others were tucked up safe at home

"Check out that fanatic sky," he said, craning his head to see.

"A storm's coming fast."

"Beautiful, isn't it?" He kept on driving toward the darkness. "Just like a fantastic stream of poetry, twisting and turning through shadows and sunlight. Like I was saying, you got to have a story, girl. In a yarn it can't be all this niceness—you know, like the two of us going out for all these months, and nothing bad ever happening except a few arguments about tales or some little thing. Something has to happen. Has to crack open the husk of their sweetness-and-light world and let some formless, soon-to-be-grasped shape out or in."

"You didn't think enough happened in my story?"

"It had fine parts and the writing was smooth, but nothing ever happened. The teacher just stayed in one place and taught her students and was a little sad when they left, though they probably never thought about her again."

"I don't know. Maybe that was the truth of the way it was for her. What's more, my teachers meant a lot to me, and I want to mean something to my students. I really love teaching speech classes and directing plays. You didn't like school, but I did."

"Hell, yes, I hated most of it! And I despised the bumpkins who thought they could tell me what to do." He raked a hand through his hair, setting it on end. "But what I'm saying is that a lot more needs to happen—a whole lot more. You remember the story about the Mongol boy whose bride was stolen by his best friend? It's a story I've told plenty of times. Because in it something happens worth the telling. And it wasn't just because he had that gorgeous poem of a horse, too, all white and jeweled, with wings to carry him up into the ether."

"He was a poet, I guess."

"That's what I think, too," Conall said, shifting in his seat and pointing off to the north, where a wide band slanting down from the clouds meant it was raining over much of the next county. "He and his girl were happy. They saw each other all the time, and they were in love, though maybe they didn't say it. Didn't need to say the words because it was so clear that they were meant for each other. Her parents liked him. Their engagement was grade-A bliss. It makes a terrible story."

"But maybe it doesn't have to be. Maybe a story could be just the boy walking all that long way to her house—because the horse wasn't real, except for being poetry—and making up Mongol songs along the way." Maybelline shrugged and leaned against the car door to peer up at the sky.

"But that's just nothing—"

"And if his friend stole his girl and ran off, maybe the Mongol boy would still invent that horse-head thing—"

"The morin khuur," Conall burst out, leaning toward the wheel.

"And sing to her parents," she finished.

"The morin khuur is the national instrument of Mongolia," he said. "It is very important to the people."

"Yes," she said, "I remember now."

"And that story would still be nothing, Maybelline. Don't you see that?"

"I still don't see why a tale has to have so much thrashing about in it—all these nutty problems that people don't have around here. It's as though a story were a Mexican jumping bean, and inside is some horrible larval thing that's trying to get out. But hardly anybody ever stumbles on a buried city or a labyrinth. Nobody ever finds magical snakes sneaking through the ground. Nobody ever tries to steal somebody's soul."

"Oh, I don't know. Seems to me like rattlesnakes are always magically underfoot in Texas. And I don't know about you, but these gourd-headed people are always sneaking around, trying to find and steal my soul. They want to bottle it up somehow, so that I can't get out. And labyrinths? Labyrinths are funny places. A job at the five-and-dime can mean being shut up in a too-symmetrical labyrinth, needing to find a way out. A family tree can look like a drawing of a maze, all disorderly and full of dead ends and hushed-up horrors. Even a prairie or a desert can be a labyrinth, if you look at it right. Lots of people are caught in one and can't find their way out, or don't like the only path out. Maybe I'm one of those people."

Maybelline made a gesture as though throwing off unrealistic dilemmas.

"But I don't know why the Mongol boy didn't tell her that he loved her. Some people seem to think that they want to be loved and should be loved, yet they never bother saying the words to anybody else. In the end they miss out. Somebody else comes along who's willing to say those words." She thumped her hand against the door in emphasis.

"But, Maybelline—"

She interrupted. "I think maybe the girl got tired of wondering whether the boy loved her after all. Maybe that's what happened with the friend. Maybe she went away with him of her own free will, and there wasn't any butchering of a horse with wings. The Mongol boy's friend bumped into her at the general store, where she was buying some feed for her pet lamb, and he told the girl that he loved her, that he had always loved her and been secretly jealous of his friend. And even though she loved her sweetheart, her heart was stirred, and she went away with the friend because she needed to hear somebody say those words."

Conall pressed on the gas pedal, and the car surged forward.

"Now you're just being silly, Maybelline. There wouldn't be any tale at all if that was what happened. Mongolians wouldn't bother passing down the legend of the morin khuur because there wouldn't be any point. I mean, where's the interest? Where's the story if she went along of her own free will?"

Conall pointed to a straw-colored streak in the distance. "See there? Coyote. A coyote's as strange as a monster from the deeps. The world's a queer place. The thing is, even if there's a cursed ruin or a tortured soldier or maybe a mad, gibbering soul from a crypt, people feel the story just as much—probably a whole hell of a lot more—as if it were an account of a teacher struggling with her superintendent over how she's going to run her class. A lot of men do, anyway. They feel my stories just like a lightning strike, branding them and setting them on fire. It digs down into the old, eternal male that's buried under a cairn of stone but biding his time in the grave—or maybe under the whole tacky veneer of civilization that's laid over the ancient drumbeating heart of wildness and vigor."

"I can't do anything about not being born a boy," she said. "I'm glad I was born a girl."

"Thank God. If anybody has the fire of a hero, it's you. But I like you better in a skirt."

Maybelline frowned at the vanishing coyote. "Those things aren't real to me, Conall. A Mongol boy who loses his girl because he never tells her he loves her—there, that's real to me. That could just as easily be a Texas story."

"And who says a white horse with wings isn't real? If it's in the story, well, there the hell it is. See, a flying stallion could be as real as a talking serpent who offers a woman an apple off the tree of knowledge. It may suggest or stand for or be a symbol of something else as well, but it's still a damn talking serpent or a flying horse in a story. Hellfire, girl, would you know a flying horse if he picked you up and sailed you over a pecan tree?"

"I don't think that's too likely. Nothing at all like that has ever happened or ever will happen in Texas, I imagine."

"Maybe not, but tornadoes have plucked people up and plunked them down easy somewhere else—or hurled them down dead."

"More commonly the latter, don't you think?"

He stopped the car on a rise in the ground and twisted to face her. "It's not the happy, contented days that make the story of the Mongol boy. Not even when there's an argument, and the boy and his girl fight over something or other. It's not even him walking around making up poems and tales and—"

"The sky's getting pretty dark," she broke in.

"Magnificent, isn't it?" He gazed off in the distance where the deep blue mounting up in the sky and trailing streamers of rain and cloud looked like a gigantic man o' war surrounded by jellyfish.

"Maybe we'd better head back."

"In a minute," he said. "Let's just get out and stand in the wind before we go." Before she could reply, he had jumped out and wrenched open her door.

"Conall," she said, "you are sure-enough crazy after all."

"That's what they say about me," he boomed, the blast of wind tumbling his words away.

"I take back all those times I defended you against hidebound, pea-brained people in town," she shouted, staggering from the car.

The wind shoved at them, hurling Conall's tie over his shoulder, making Maybelline stumble against his chest. Bending, he kissed her on the mouth, feeling passion that was swirled together with the barbaric ink of the sky and the impetuousness of the winds. She might be a naiad or a Greek girl about to be transformed into a lithe tree. Already her dress fluttered wildly against her body, as if the silk had been changed to a frenzy of cottonwood leaves. Yielding, she slipped her arms around his neck and kissed him before turning her face away, staring at the turbulent sky.

The storm looked closer and more threatening. Medusa clouds climbed higher, at times briefly metamorphosing into even stranger creatures of the sea as they streamed on fast currents of air. The landscape yielded to their shadows.

"Just look at that colossal thing," he shouted, gesturing as she broke away from him, turning to face the wind.

An enormous twisted tree seemed bleached against the deep blue backdrop. In all the landscape, it was the sole shape that shone out, dominating the scrub and the flat land and the hillock where the car was parked.

"Can't you see grotesque shadows out of the past creeping across that ground or a barbarian man arrowing swiftly away from the storm, heading for shelter in the rocks, maybe pursued by his enemy? Or maybe it's a girl, fleeing from a man, the hair on her head prickling with static. Imagine that Mongol boy spiraling around the tree in a storm—or crossing the plain and in the flash from a stab of lightning, finding his horse butchered on the ground, the blood clotted like jam on the wings." Conall's face looked ecstatic as the gust whipped his hair from side to side.

"I can see me and you frizzled by a big lightning strike," Maybelline yelled. "Does that count? Let's get out of here!"

He waved his arms at the boiling mass of cloud and the delicate tentacles swaying below. "The Mongols think the Northern sky spirit, Keiden Khan, brought the lightning and rough weather. A meteorite or anything struck by lightning has power and is called *tengeriin us*, the hair of heaven."

Maybelline gripped his arm. "Conall, stop it! You and me, we're going to be heaven's hair if we don't get the hell out of this place!"

A pale volcanic fire seethed among the jellyfish, and with a burst of electricity that invaded burrows and set the fur of animals on end for miles around, a massive bolt struck the upper branches of the tree and raged downward. Brightness cabled the silhouette in white gold. For a split instant the skeletal shape burned on the retina before exploding into a blaze, just as a gigantic *CRACK!* sundered the air. In jittery flashes, the scrub around the bonfire tree shone a dead white. Momentarily, the tree appeared to withstand the force of the strike and remain intact, but then either the jolt or some inner combustion cleaved the trunk in two, and a globe of fire streaked from its heart, igniting dry shrubs and tumbleweeds as it bowled forward.

Unable to stir but feeling the enormity of slammed lightning echo in their ears, the two watchers stared at each other, shocked and unable to speak. Maybelline was trembling.

Fistfuls of fat drops struck them in the face and spattered their arms.

As if an enormous trap door in the heavens had been wrenched open, a downburst slammed against the earth.

Mammy

"If there's one thing I like, it's a nice big slab of cake. I don't mind if I have another one, thank you, ma'am."

Conall lifted his glass of milk and added, "To Maybelline's Mammy, who rustles up the best cakes in Texas!" After he drank and put down the glass, his milk mustache made the women laugh. "I sure do like coming to visit you all on the farm, Mammy, because I know there's going to be good talk and good grub."

"And I like it when you come here to visit because you know how to flatter a cook," she returned.

Maybelline and her grandmother and Conall were sitting at the dining room table, close to a red velvet cake on a green glass stand and a pitcher of milk fresh from the springhouse, its cheek dewy with moisture. Mammy had fetched one of her mother's tablecloths in honor of the guest, linen embroidered with purple passion flowers and green maypops, with the legend of the passion flower stitched in black thread along the hem. On the wall hung a pair of violins made of cobalt glass, and on the sideboard in the place of honor stood a large glass cylinder with intaglio medallions and putti and bold relief cutting, with a pineapple finial on the lid.

"That's beautiful old glass," Conall said. "It really sparkles in the sunlight. A lot of craftsmanship must go into a piece like that."

"Oh, yes," Mammy said, "all that glass-blowing and then the cutting and grinding of those rows of ovals and rings and leaves. And then carving out cherubs carrying palm leaves and medallions with somebody's coat of arms, I guess. The glassworkers must have had patience. It's old, that glass. More than two hundred years, maybe. Daddy told me it was made in Brandenburg."

"Brandenburg," Conall said. "Where did you get such a marvel?"

"The jar came down to me from my father, who received it as a bequest from his closest friend, a Mr. Lee Roy Lamb, back in Georgia. That's where I grew up. The piece survived the war between the states by being wrapped in rags and buried in the ground."

"Mammy's father called it *The Lazarus Jar* because the glass rose from the grave," Maybelline said.

"That's right," Mammy said. "The Lambs didn't dig up their family treasures until the fighting had been over a long time. After the war came a bad patch, and so they just waited. His wife, Miss Mary, was afraid to have anything valuable in the house. Before the war, they had a lot of gold coins, and they kept them buried, too, until some years after, when Georgia was a bit safer and his eldest child was old enough to be responsible."

Conall rubbed a finger along the condensed drops on the side of his glass. Cool rivulets ran down and soaked the cloth. "So the valuables were all still there when they dug it up?"

Mammy nodded. "My father and Mr. Lee Roy Lamb's boy built a shed over the place where the gold was buried. It wasn't a very elegant thing, not like what Mr. Lamb could have done, but it was enough to keep off prying eyes while they dug. I held the lantern when they hauled up the bundles, and I can remember Mr. Lamb holding the jar in his arms just like it was a baby wrapped in dirty swaddling clothes, with his fingers pushing aside the rags and caressing that concave medallion in the center. Lee Roy Lamb, Jr., was only fourteen or fifteen at the time."

"Why didn't the father just dig it up himself? Why didn't he build the shed?" Conall took another bite of cake.

"He was blinder than a skillet. He was just as blind as blind could be. But not always. Before the war, he had inherited some money and valuables from an uncle in England, and he became a house builder. Mr. Lamb was a good saver, but he never trusted anything but gold. He was a careful man, and only he and his wife knew where their goods were buried. The Lambs had just the one son and three daughters, all of them younger than their brother."

Mammy's hands went on pleating the napkin and then tucking it under the edge of her plate, but she looked out the window at the leafless trees and the chicken house beyond.

"It was because of the war that he was blind," she said.

The room was quiet for a few moments. Then Conall asked, "Was he shot?"

"Well, he had been shot, somewhere up in Virginia, and he took bad sick with the wound. He was lucky not to die. Some said he should have, and saved himself from what came later on."

Mammy stopped for a moment, her hand resting on an embroidered flower. Her fingertips touched the French knots at the center, as if reading a message from the past.

"My father always said Mr. Lamb was against secession, but he defended his home and went to war like the rest. After a time, he came back with a peg leg, but he got around all right and could do a little carpentry. He made a false wall in our pantry with a puzzle latch, so we could hide our food, and he did the same for a few others who were close friends. You didn't want a thing like that to get around, or the soldiers would be tearing down the houses to get at secret stores. There wasn't any call for new construction, though he did help raise a two-room box for some neighbors who were burned out by the Yankees."

"What an awful thing! They torched the house?" Conall leaned forward, the fork held tightly in his fist.

"Oh, yes, they burned it out of pure meanness, I believe," Mammy said. "Some boys came through fixing to make mischief. They weren't with a company, though they had on uniforms. Maybe they never were soldiers at all."

"What happened to the family?" Conall was as intent on the answer as if the remains of the timbers were still smoldering.

Mammy took a sip of milk and sat back in her chair, gazing out the window once more.

"Some of the children were still inside when they set the house ablaze. One of the little boys jumped from the second story into his brother's arms. The mother had a weak heart and was lying out in the yard in a dead faint, the younger ones howling around her. My friend Elizabeth Ann was the bravest one. When she saw her mama laid out like a log and no big brother in sight (he was around back, I guess, catching that boy), she hiked up her skirts and dashed inside and fetched the baby from his cradle in the parlor. Got a bad burn on her arm, and when it healed, the skin was puckered. Later on, Miss Mary told her it was a beauty mark."

"A beauty mark," Conall repeated. "Were they all right afterward?"

She shrugged slightly, as if to ask what *all right* could mean in such days.

"The family—they were Jarriels—slept in the barn for a while, until the little one took sick. Mr. Lamb and some of the neighborhood women and children had been building them a house, but the work was too slow to save the baby. After that, the Jarriels stayed in the summer kitchen. You got to watch out about sleeping where there's hay because it can go bad and make you sick."

Mammy looked down at the embroidered passion flowers on the tablecloth.

"My mother was a fine needlewoman, but she got to be right good with a hammer that year."

"God, that's dreadful!" Conall's fork clashed against the plate. "And you remember the smoke going up, and your friend saving the baby? That's like what a boom does to a town, only worse. Maybe war is a kind of boom that lets loose the scavengers and murderers and unlocks the evil in men's hearts. How can things like that be allowed? How can men bear what they are and how the world is?"

"That was a sad time," Mammy said. "Everybody says that war is terrible, but you don't know how bad it is until you see the children hungry and carrying on because they got word that their daddy won't ever come home, and the women struggling to keep the family together and bring in a crop for some two-legged varmint to steal. Strangers would come through and butcher a cow or take the last bag of meal, and if a child set up a fuss, he might be knocked down or worse. Girls didn't go out alone. It wasn't safe."

Conall trembled with anger. "Men are savages," he said. "They have a grain of hatred deep inside."

He pressed one hand against his chest, knowing that he, too, was seeded with that ancient hate. Hadn't he felt tendrils breaking free of the seed coat—a black flower that didn't bear examining in the light—felt them in the safety of his own kitchen, sitting next to the woman who had given birth to him at the risk of her own life and later taught him to read and write? If a man wasn't free from the dark seed in the one place he belonged, surely he was free nowhere.

His eyes rested on the cut glass jar, as if he could find, in all the hundreds of facets, some gleam of an answer as to why.

"Mammy, tell him how Mr. Lamb became blind." Maybelline touched her grandmother's arm.

She nodded, cutting another piece of cake and passing the plate to Conall. "You better eat up this cake because it might be a while before you get another one."

He cut into the slice, his thoughts moving slowly away from a burning house, lost in time, somewhere in Georgia.

"Yes," he said, "tell us."

"People kept speculating that Mr. Lee Roy Lamb had some gold and silver hidden—he had been so well off before the war—but he always laughed and said that he didn't have anything but Confederate money, and it had been used for paper in the outhouse. The truth was, he had coin money and a silver service and bowls, and some fancy old glass like that jar, all of them buried in the ground."

Mammy picked up her napkin again and, after a moment, began twisting it into a rope.

"A party of lowlifes straggled through town, hunting up trouble—this was not long after the war had ended, but most of our men hadn't come home to Georgia. Some of them had been penned up in New York and Ohio prison camps, and some were dead. Some of the deceased we knew about, and some we didn't. So the women had to be strong without their men because the fellows who came trickling through the countryside were a scabby lot. Sometimes it was hard to tell camp followers from soldiers, unless they were with their own units. Gangs roamed around, causing havoc—probably the same sort of vultures who used to strip the dead of anything they had of value, any decent parts of uniforms or watches or rings. Sometimes they'd leave those poor boys naked of everything but photographs or a Bible or letters. Didn't have any use for those. The ones who came searching after the Lambs were nothing but riff-raff."

Mammy looked at the twisted napkin in her hands as if wondering how it had gotten that way. She set it to one side of her plate and continued her story.

"Somehow they heard that Mr. Lee Roy Lamb had gold, so they hunted him down and questioned him in the kitchen, but he denied it. His little son was calling through the door, and when his mama came to fetch him with a baby in her arms, one of the men opened the door and grinned with his nasty rotten teeth and touched her on the breast so that she shrieked, and that set the children a-crying. At this, Mr. Lee Roy Lamb got very wroth, but the men had the upper hand and knocked him flat. One of them put a poker in the fire. When the metal was red-hot, they waved it around and threatened him, trying to scare out of him the place where the gold was hidden. Mrs. Lamb took the children and left the house on foot to get help because she was afraid they would all be slaughtered. My mother could hear her tearing through the fields, screams jolting out of her as she ran. Mama took her to town in the wagon—we still had an old played-out mule that looked too bony to eat—but two hours passed before she got back with help. By then the strangers had stripped the beds and stolen what little was in the pantry."

Mammy stopped to wipe her eyes with the hem of her apron.

"In the kitchen Mr. Lee Roy Lamb had been left on the floor, his eyes burned out with the red hot poker. Lord have mercy, those men had no more heart than to sizzle the gel right out of his head."

"Oh, my God, how horrible!" Conall stood up from the table, stared around the room as if bewildered, and then sat back down. "Did they ever catch those men? Did they ever punish them? Hanging would be too kind for such wolves!"

Mammy shook her head. "No, I don't believe a one of those roisterers was ever caught. It seems like they were tracked to their next stop or two, but then they slipped the noose. They probably went whistling home safe and sound after the war, if they had such a thing as a place to go. And if any of them had a wife, they probably beat her by way of a howdy. They were nothing but the worse kind of scum."

Conall gripped the fork between his fingers, the slice of cake forgotten.

"Sometimes I suspect there's nothing much but rascals, North or South," he said. "That's why I learned to fight and made myself strong enough to clobber the trash in town. Back then, I felt sure that I'd never be afraid of anything if I could box."

He glanced up at the glass jar.

"Were his eyes worth some silver and gold and family treasures?"

"Those men were after meanness. They probably would have put his eyes out anyway," Mammy said. "You know, the jar reminds me of those scoundrels, but it also reminds me of Mr. Lee Roy Lamb and his family. They were a solid, prayerful kind of people. After he was blinded, he kept on as a carpenter, making boxes and chests by touch. The things were right pretty. He would get my daddy to help him pick out the different colors of wood for each one. Used to put a little code of scratches on the end of a board that told him the type. Some of the grains he could recognize by the feel. I've got a little jewelry box he made from pecan burl."

"Mammy, you're a real storyteller," Conall said, now digging into his cake. "But I don't see how you can stand those memories. Seems to me you'd want to rid the world of all men-varmints."

"You don't see too many of them around my farm. Nothing but a rooster." She gave the table a quick slap for emphasis.

"You are one strong, straight woman, and I believe you can fend for yourself, Mammy. The snakes on legs and the ones that rattle had better watch out for somebody like you. So I sure am glad you let me come out with Maybelline and eat some of your good cooking."

Mammy laughed. "You aren't a fool or a snake!"

"He'd better not be," Maybelline said, smiling at him.

"Don't you go and tump over that glass of milk, now." Mammy waggled a finger at him.

"Tump! That's a good old word. You know, I wouldn't mind just a splash more," Conall said, holding out his glass for a refill.

"You just go right ahead and enjoy it." She poured the milk to the very lip of the glass.

"Yes'm," he said.

He began to eat faster, the colors and movements of Mammy's story jostling in his head.

"I don't hold anything against men in general," Mammy added, "not even Yankees. The world's fallen, just as smashed as a pretty little blue-and-green glass bowl dropped on flagstones. Most people go around heedless, not paying any mind to what the good Lord wants for them. They don't care a fig about loving God or their fellow man. Go galloping after your own self and what you think and want, and you sure won't end up anywhere but the land of havoc."

"Amen, Mammy." Maybelline got up from the table and gave her grandmother a hug. "That's better preaching than I've heard in church."

Conall wasn't listening, his thoughts having flown to an image of a face with burned-out craters than had once been eyes.

King of the Pulps

Conall was walking off the evening's upset, every now and then giving a jab of the hand as if he were boxing, though he hadn't boxed in a long time. In boxers' years, he was well on to being washed up, or so he told himself.

She had flown at him!

She had flown at him like a sparrow bedeviling a hawk, hectoring and dive-bombing him without mercy!

He couldn't understand it.

He couldn't wrap his mind around why she had been so angry at him.

"I should've just gotten her a damn diamond," he muttered.

And she hadn't even showed the book to anyone! She had hidden the volume underneath some papers in a suitcase, so that Mammy and her mother wouldn't look inside. The truth was that he had never thought about either one of them wanting to read those stories, and he'd been proud of ordering her such an expensive and downright pretty book, the complete works of Pierre Louÿs, all in one volume. But she had been ashamed for either one of them to see his gift and said that her mother would have forbidden her to see him again if she had known.

He had never thought that she would be offended. She was a writer, damn it to hell! She had to be open to the truth of things, or what was the use?

"Do no wrong to thy neighbor. Observing this, do as thou pleaseth." What kind of motto was that, she had wanted to know. *Do as thou pleaseth?* Wasn't that just what her Mammy had been talking about? Wasn't that just what had made some carousing men shove a red hot poker into Mr. Lee Roy Lamb's eyes, so that the jelly sputtered and bubbled and died along the iron? Wasn't that what had made the boomtown years so terrible, the streets alive with scavengers and whores and vermin?

He had never heard her talk that way!

And he couldn't remember anything her precious Mammy had said about doing or not doing what one pleased, though he remembered so clearly the riff-raff who came looking for Georgia gold and left a man on the floor, blinded.

Maybelline...

He felt humiliated. Rushing along in the dark, he wanted to end everything. *You damn fool, you damn fool, you worthless damn fool.* He wanted to throw himself under the car that passed, the driver veering onto the opposite side of the road when he lunged forward. Maybelline just didn't understand sex, though she was the closest thing to a soulmate that he had ever found. Hadn't she come to him like a great wash of vitality and spirit?

Still, she was right. She knew how people were, and somehow he didn't—didn't know what was proper to say and do. He was fine with the old ones, because they loved it when somebody wanted to hear tales of the lost days, gone by forever. But mostly he was nothing but a bull in a china shop, breaking and smashing and stepping on glazed delicacies. He was not decorous. He was not genteel.

She was disgusted by Louÿs, by his "bawdy and good-natured sovereign" King Pausole, by the king's harem of a thousand wives, by his daughter "the pure Aline" who tiptoed away from the castle with a boy lover who was really a girl in disguise, by his giant Eunuch, by Mirabelle, by Giguelillot.

Oh, she had noticed the elegance of style, all right. She was enough of a writer for that. But she wasn't impressed that Louÿs was a cohort of Gide and Wilde or that some of his songs had been set to music by his friend Debussy. No, she was not one to be swayed by a fine name.

She had made it absolutely clear to Conall that no beau in small-town Texas or anywhere else on the face of North America—maybe in France, sure!—ought to give his girl a book containing a poem where a naked girl, her heels reddened by crushed petals, rides the branch of a tree or where a woman offers her breasts to another like a pair of white pigeons to a goddess or powders them with the pollen from flowers. A torrent of images had flooded into his mind as she made her distaste known.

As solid and sharp as the quartz crystal in his pocket was the news that she did not want to read poems that hung a little naked Astarte around the neck of a slender girl—a girl caressed by a naked woman who offered their twin Astartes (for a tiny idol dangled between the breasts of each) lovely pink roses. No, Maybelline did not wish to hear about a woman's grief for her lost lover, recalled as seated in an auroral dusting of powder, hair pinned up, and retouching the red of her lips with a delicate finger. The songs that Bilitis had written on petals and leaves and scraps of vellum were not suitable gifts.

Yes, she had skimmed here and there in the book and read some lovely descriptions of the lacy, frost-encrusted woods and the chunks of ice lifted to a pale sky in order to see the tomb of the naiads. The strangeness of that world—the bustle of Mytilene, the rosette- or boat-shaped gold earrings, the perfumed hair of men and of women, the purple and hyacinth tunics, the saddle cloths with threads of gold, the stalls of amber and ivory jewelry, the flutes—was appealing, just as fragments of another world seen in a museum case would be. Like-

Maze of Blood

wise, she found the tomb of Bilitis curious, the walls covered with plaques of black amphibolite, the terra cotta coffin, the vials of perfume and the mirror, the stylus with which the dead woman had once spread blue paint on her eyelids, the golden jewels on the skeleton "white as a branch of snow" and as frail, falling to dust when touched.

Yet none of the classical polish and the evocation of a lost world had pleased her because the whole was "too sensuous, unclean." A man didn't—or shouldn't—give such a thing to his sweetheart for a Christmas gift.

He still wasn't sure whether she had been more offended by the sapphic passages or by the idea of a girl worshipping Astarte.

In vain he had argued that this was the way the world was headed and that he and she could do nothing about it. In vain he urged her to examine her own erotic, luxury-loving civilization. As a writer, how could she do otherwise? She did not believe him. Texas was not like that, she told him. Most people went to work and church and did their best to raise their children to be good and true.

He walked faster, swinging his arms.

She was an innocent, a sealed bud. He felt coming change over-shadowing all, and it wasn't simply a more wanton time rolling toward them. Cataclysm approached. Clashes involving race and religion and degree of wealth had come before and would come again. The Western world was setting like a star, and she would see that he was right. Untrammeled sex and boom-times luxury would rule. Opulence and splendor would corrupt. From the East, hordes would rage across nations, bent on destruction, and drag Europe and America into barbarism. The whole damnable wheel of fortune would keep on rolling. King one moment, fool the next—the wheel meant revolution of mind and body. A person could do nothing except try not to be crushed. Flux was the nature of human history.

He didn't want to lose her.

But he was a man of the prairie, and his art flowered like a tall yucca stalk, a sun-loving phallus. Out of anger he had told her that he owned a vaquero heart, saying, "Cowboys don't let women tie them down."

(Maeve had hated it when he played cowboys and Indians with other boys. She didn't care for Indians—the old pioneer stock in her flinched from the bare idea of them—and she thought that his girl looked to have Indian blood, with her olive skin and dark hair and eyes. "A nut-brown maid," she said, like in the old song.)

Still stung by Maybelline's aversion, he had repeated the words, *Cowboys don't let women tie them down.*

She had made a stupid joke about that—something about how the cowboys were therefore safe from old Pierre Louÿs—and informed him of all the labor wives and mothers had to do, whether they were teachers or not, and how that wasn't so all-fired free and easy. Was he sure about who tied whom, she wanted to know.

He trudged up the road toward home.

It was all ashes, all damn ashes, his stories and poems and everything. If he didn't have them and her, what did he have? His mother had loved him without stint, had claimed him in the rolling cataract of her love and refused to let go, but she would die and leave him alone, save for his father—and that was not enough for him, to see Doc off in the distance, shaking hands, or coming home to rock and drift to sleep in his chair.

The pair of them had tried to deny death. When his mother lost a baby, they swept the place over and pretended that death did not exist, just as later they covered over Caradog and harrowed the back lot. Yet all his life, mortality had been with him, peering out of his mother's eyes, speaking in tubercular coughs, manifesting its power in phlegm and blood. His parents had tried to pretend it was not so, and he had pretended alongside to please them.

When he banged open the screen door, they were ensconced in the living room, settled in their usual places.

Maze of Blood

"Fletcher's here," his mother said, and his old friend rose from a chair.

"Good to see you! Come on back, come on back," Conall called. "I've just been taking a breather. I needed a walk and some fresh air."

The show of heartiness sounded false to his ear, but he led the way to his room and switched on the lamp. The space seemed smaller than it had when they were boys.

Fletcher sat on the edge of the bed. The magazines stacked in heaps on the coverlet shifted, showing their colors.

"You still seeing Maybelline?"

His friend didn't wait for an answer, the brightness of the pulps demanding that he at least ruffle through a heap of them, fanning them across the bed.

"Would you look at these magazines! How'd you get your name plastered on all these covers? You are the king of the pulps, that's what you are. The greatest writer of pulp fiction alive! And I was there when you got your first big acceptance. Hard to believe how many stories you've published since then."

"I'm dating her, sure." Conall sat down, turning the chair to face Fletcher.

"And you've kept up writing to Wildsmith and that circle?"

Conall nodded. "I get letters from writers all the time now. It's funny. I'm like a different person with them. Paper friends aren't like flesh-and-blood friends. There's a thing or two that your friends understand, yet you can't begin to explain to somebody who's never been to some piddling town in Texas. Sometimes I feel like the me in the letters is made up. A character in a story. Different. I get letters from a lot of readers, too. It makes me feel pretty good, like I belong to some crazy tribe of bards and fans who give a damn whether I live or die."

Fletcher flipped through one of the magazines, stopping when he found Conall's name. "How's the story-writing going? Swell, I guess."

"Some of the pulps don't pay up any too fast," Conall said. "That's pretty damn annoying. But it's all right otherwise. I crank one out and start another. My rigamarole's gotten pretty popular, and I've been mulling some ideas for a book."

"I never pictured you going with a schoolteacher," Fletcher said, "but Maybelline sure does love to read and write, and she's got more life in her pinkie than most people have in their whole body."

"Never pictured me with anybody would be more like it. Who'd want a great Texas galoot like me? That's what came to my mind. I'm nothing but a pariah in this godforsaken hole."

"Probably you could have a string of girls who would like to date a Texas galoot if you moved to a city. Think about all those fan letters. Some of those are bound to be from women. You bought Maybelline a ring yet?"

"No. Not this Christmas. She'd rather have a big fancy book than a diamond. Can you feature that? She's the girl for me, all right. I got her a special book, too."

Conall stared at his hands.

"I really wish she didn't care so much about school. It's getting in the way of her writing. She's got real talent, and she's bound to write tales that sell, sooner or later. But she puts a lot of herself into these kids who don't actually give a damn about her—won't remember her name in ten years. She stays up all hours directing plays and grading papers."

"Nothing wrong with a teacher who cares," Fletcher said.

"I can't picture anybody liking it well enough to spend that kind of time," Conall admitted. "Maybe that's just me. I hated school a lot of the time. There were some good things, but they were mostly our doing—the school paper and magazines were fine, but I could have skipped most of the rest without shedding any tears. You wouldn't believe the rules the superintendent lays on the teachers! They've got to be role models around the clock. Teachers can't drink or smoke, dance or play bridge, stay out late—I don't know what all. Who'd give a damn if somebody played bridge?"

"The school board, I guess."

Conall lowered his voice. "You know how I'm not free to do what I like. Not about Maybelline. Not yet."

"Yeah, I know." Fletcher nodded, unsmiling now.

"My mother's not doing so well these days. I feel damn sorry for her, clinging to her scrap of life. She's fought that old TB so long, and done better than Doc ever thought she could, but now she's just about helpless."

"She's had a bad time of it, all right," Fletcher said. "Can you slip out for a while? What do you say we get a beer or two and go down to the icehouse?"

"Sure. I haven't been by there in a long while."

Conall got up from the chair. Reaching for the coin he had been flung, long ago in New Orleans, he shoved it deep in his pocket. He was feeling easier now, though his mind kept looping around to Maybelline and the terrible thought that he was a damn fool, nothing, nothing, nothing but a damn fool.

The Chimæran

Hemen put his hand over the schoolteacher's mouth and stripped away the straight skirt and slip, the damp-footed stockings and the garter belt that he held up like a prize, wondering what use he could make of such a thing, the harness of the bra under the skein of blouse that he fingered, intrigued by its delicately wrinkled surface.

"It's called *crepe*," the teacher whispered. She had twisted her face away from his hand, yet she couldn't stop teaching, even at a time like this.

"No talk," grunted the barbarian, stripping away the last vestige of civilization from the woman's body. Naked, she seemed impossibly pale and fragrant and pure, marked only by a fading colorless tattoo left by the pressure of fabric and seams.

He slid into her as into the thousand rain forests of adventure. Underneath the thin cloth she was as wild as any, and he began to run silently.

"I'm—"

"No," he panted, closing his eyes.

A bird razored across the path, crying out in womanish shrieks.

Then Hemen broke through to a deeper layer of woods, a drenched world where leaves slapped against his arms. Giant blossoms spilled their water onto his head as he raced on through the gloom, veering to avoid the disasters of slippery waterfalls or unexpected downed trunks. Crom! The Picts were after him now, the ominous murmur of passage coming to him faintly. Why had any of them left their cold, bitter lands, each pursuing the other to this hot place? Faster, faster: the heart in his chest panicked like a fish in a basket trap. Muscles tautened as he surged forward, knowing that he could make it, he could reach the high falls and pass through sunless underground caverns back to the light.

He saw them now, the blue haze of their tattoos like shadows among the leaves. How could it be that death was hiding in the trees when he was a star rover burning with life? He heard the *twang!* of the greased tendon and the *thwock* of the shaft burying itself in his flesh.

"Did—"

"Hush!" he ejaculated.

His star went nova. Life burst from him like the falls just ahead, unreachable, jolting into the sunshine.

Caddo

It was a mistake for them to stop at one of the Caddo Peaks. She didn't have the right shoes for the walk to the hill or for the path up—not that either of the low mountains was such a tough climb, but soft leather pumps weren't meant for sand and dirt and stone.

Why did women wear such damnable footwear?

She went ahead anyway, grabbing onto trees and scrub and him until they reached one of the spots where he used to play and dig when he was a boy. Now it looked oddly like a grave that had been open a long time, the sides worn by the wind and slippage of the sandstone as it crumbled into fragments or trickled downward as fine powder.

On the path he had told her about his time with Vortigern, how the warlord king had welcomed the Angles and Saxons to Britain, a decision that proved to be a fatal error of judgment and led to bloodshed. In this prior life, Conall had fought with Vortigern and the Britons against Saxon armies under the rebellious mercenary leaders, Horsa and Hengest. During the first battle he had received a slash to the face and skull that should have killed him, and afterward he was not much good as a fighter.

Carried away by the story, he had even added something that he was sure he did not remember, though he liked it—how the high king had retreated to a hill in northern Wales and built a fortified castle there.

"In the morning we would start out and lever the stones into place. With so many of us, the work on the two towers moved along steadily. We heaped dirt outside the first rows of stone and set another row. By nightfall we were exhausted and lay flopped like dead men under the trees. In the morning the towers would be rubble. Every morning the same."

"What terrible great fools to keep building them, then." Maybelline stopped and emptied silt from her shoes.

"Oh, well, maybe. Do you want to hear what happened next?" He didn't wait for a reply. "The high king sent his men to search for a fairy child who was to set the thing right, and they found him in Carmarthen. His name was Myrddin Emrys, and he gave them the secret. Two dragons were battling in an underground pool—"

"My feet hurt," she announced.

That's when they stopped by the grave, and he helped her down to the ground in her straight skirt that was no good for climbing. He even rubbed her feet while she looked at the view, though much of it was blocked by an unfortunately placed tree, and told her more about *Myrddin Emrys*, or Merlin.

She interrupted him.

"Didn't you tell me the king of the Britons committed incest with his own daughter? And was struck by lightning for his evil deeds? I don't like this fellow Vortigern."

"It was the fifth century AD, so there's a lot we don't know. Those might have been lies put about by enemies. But I never said he was nice. I said he was interesting, Maybelline." He stared at her and began to laugh.

She laughed with him and leaned her head on his arm.

"See," she said, "I want some beauty all tied up with goodness and truth in a story, even if it's a bleak, sad tale. Why don't you write that novel about Texas you talked about, with real history and real places? Why does it always have to be palaces and secret hiding places containing Merlin's gold chair and Merlin's gold chest of who-knows-what? Why do women have to be halfway to Lilith and never normal old Eve? Why does it have to be elemental man against elemental man? Why is it always the barbarians overrunning a decadent civilization?"

"Because that's how it is! Hell, civilization is delicate, easily smashed. And then the barbarians come. Always. Besides, I've written stories about Texas," he said, looking into the smoothed-out pit where he used to search for fossils.

"Funny stories, mostly. Write a serious story about the cowboys and frontiersmen and men and women who farm the land or the little towns where people don't have anything much but one another and grit. That striving against obstacles to make a life—it's hard but full of truth and hope. If you put it in words, the beauty and longing for something more would creep in."

He reached down, rubbing around the place where a fingerling of fossil shone.

"I don't care so much about those flyspecks of towns, I guess. But I aim to write a Texas novel before I die. If I have the time, and if the oil well isn't played out. You know I'm in my sere-and-yellow leaf, girl."

She laughed at him for saying so. Perhaps he had said those words too many times. They were good words—Shakespeare's words. But he knew how that acted in a tale. You could have a character say a thing too often until it went dead and hollow.

Again it came to him that she didn't think much of his stories. Oh, she knew he was a fine writer of prose and poetry and, what was perhaps more to her, a published author. Still, she didn't care much for his rovers and kings and barbarian soldiers, and all his arabesque dreams were just armfuls of dead leaves to Maybelline. The old familiar thought came to him that he was fool, nothing but a fool.

He was quiet going down the slope, remembering to help her over the steep places but not feeling much like talk. She chattered for a while and then was silent. Somehow he wasn't sure whether it was a companionable silence.

On the flat ground below, they saw something strange, a tree full of mockingbirds, flying out and back, and a coyote running by, cackling silently with his jaws open and the tongue hanging out sideways while the birds jeered at him. Maybelline reached for his hand while they stood, watching the birds fly after the coyote and back to the tree that rustled with black-and-white wings.

"Mockingbirds don't flock, do they?"

"The world's a queer, off-kilter place," Conall said. "There's not so much common sense about it as people say there is. Any blasted thing can happen. Clouds rain minnows or frogs. Hills topple, and valleys shoot up the sky. A Texas galoot like me can have a best girl like you."

"Maybe," she said. "All I know for certain is that my feet are killing me. I guess these shoes are ruined."

"It's my fault, dragging you out to Caddo. I'll buy you some new ones in Brownwood this afternoon," he promised. "We can drive over and get the best damn pumps in town. Alligator skin, raccoon skin, lizard skin, dragon skin, or whatever the hell you want."

She didn't laugh, but she smiled.

For some time the two stood in an oval shadow of leaves and watched the mockingbirds flutter and call.

"Sometimes I can hate mockingbirds because they steal the songs from other birds," Conall said, "but that's quite a show."

"Don't they make them their own, add a bunch of curlicues and snatches of other tunes?" Maybelline slapped at her shoulder, leaving a small badge of red. "Mosquito," she said, and rubbed away the blood and fragments with a fingertip. "Maybe they're not poets dreaming up a song but just musicians, playing for the joy of it."

He kissed her then, when she must not have been expecting it, with her hurt feet and the scraped-and-scratched-up shoes dangling from one hand. Afterward, she laced her fingers with his.

"That sight was as good as a poem," Conall declared.

"Want me to recite one?"

Maybelline had often done that—she was well known around the county for recitations of poems and dramatic monologues.

"Sure," he said, and listened intently, his eyes on the birds.

He was aware that human days are rife with minor wrenches and quirks of coincidence, and perhaps this was one, no less peculiar than branches covered in mockingbirds. She chose at that moment to recite a poem that had meant a good deal to him. Conall seemed to recall her mentioning the piece before—was it when they met? But perhaps it should have been no surprise to hear her begin with the words, "Five miles meandering with a mazy motion / The sacred river ran, / Then reached the caverns measureless to man, / And sank in tumult to a lifeless ocean: / And 'mid this tumult Kubla heard from far / Ancestral voices prophesying war!" She recited the lines well, but he had heard the poem's rhythms a certain way so many times that it seemed odd to hear them changed.

When she was done, he nodded his head.

"Kubla, he was the grandson of Genghis. The khan was evidently pretty damn upset when he first saw Kubla, because the boy didn't have the red hair and greenish eyes that ran in the family."

"Well, did you like it?"

"That was wonderful. The pauses, the rhythm, and downright swing of the thing! It's about as close to perfect as anybody could get. In fact, I believe that's the second-best rendition of 'Kubla Khan' I've ever heard."

"What do you mean, second-best?"

"My mother used to recite that one for me when I was a boy. I've heard her a hundred times, probably."

She clicked her tongue and reproved him. "That's the best damn 'Kubla Khan' you ever heard! Or I'll eat an armadillo with a side dish of lizard tongues and follow it up with burrowing owl pie and stink-bug ice cream!"

At that, she set off toward the car, shoes in hand. After a few yards she paused and shoved them back on her feet.

He stood stock still, calling her name, but she kept walking.

"Would you stop? What in blue tarnation is the matter with you, Maybelline?"

When he caught up and touched her on the arm, she whirled around and pushed at him, but he crushed her body to his and kissed her. Though he had supposed that she would not, Maybelline kissed him back with warmth and even put her arms around his neck. Not letting go, he leaned back and surveyed her. The neat waves had come loose around her head, and she was perspiring.

"What happened?" He pushed a stray curl behind her ear. "I'm just a damn fool, that's all I am. I'm sorry."

She gave him a long look and then put her hand to his cheek and held it there. After a single brief note of laughter, she turned away.

"Wait," he pleaded, and reached for her fingers.

"The night we met, didn't you tell me I was a poem? That very poem?" She still faced away from him. In the sunlight, her shoulder blades showed through the thin batiste blouse.

He stood behind her, his eyes resting on a glimpse of lace, remembering.

"You're such a boy," she said, swinging back toward him. "In some ways you're a child, and all this time I was dreaming that you were a man."

As if to prove her wrong, he pulled her close and kissed her once more.

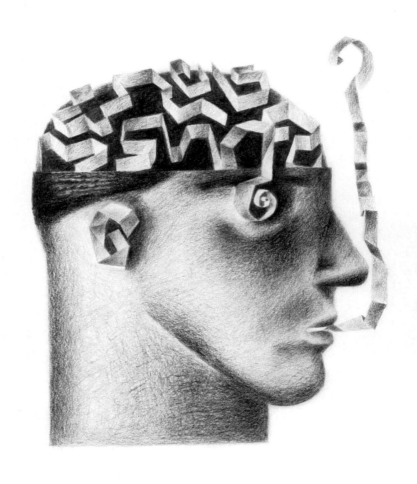

The Maze of Youth

"Nature, Hope, and Poesy"

"There's no stop to the suffering of men," Conall pronounced. A note of pomposity had come into the adolescent's voice. "The world's a wheel that rolls and tramples on human lives. A barbarian drags down the civilization that grows luxurious and forgets its soul and then begins his own climb toward decadence—and when he reaches an apex of proud, easy life, along come more barbarians to batter the gates and mow down those golden hours. And it's so, endlessly on, forever and ever, amen, because there's a seed of poison in every human being—no matter what else is there—no matter whether it's a king or a sharecropper."

Maeve's mouth was turned down at one corner, and it made her look as if she might not be listening to the long wash of words flowing over her. She and Con were shelling a mess of lady peas so tiny that it was hard to catch the bronze-colored stains that meant a sucking bug had been ramming its proboscis into the pale green flesh. One of Doc's patients had left three bushels of the long narrow pods on the porch in payment for the work of quarrying fragments of wood from an infected finger and bandaging it.

"And one man can be many men, strewn over the centuries. One time he might be a hoplite, another time a Pict with a dirk in his hand, another time a Texas Ranger. In every life he lived, he would be the same to some degree—always a warrior, always a scribe, always a bearer of burdens, or always a slave. And no matter who or what, he'd be subject to the wheel."

"What stories you tell, honey!"

"These peas are too durn small for my fingers," Conall said, throwing down a fistful of hulls.

Maeve straightened in the hard kitchen chair, holding her head high as though she had just remembered that her Celtic ancestors across the sea had worn crowns—and if not them, then their cousins, and that was close enough. "Och, and maybe that's why they were after giving them to your father. Didn't want to bother with the work." The touch of Irish slipped away. "I've got a hambone with meat on it and some onions, so I'll cook just as soon as the peas are shelled."

"I was always a bard and a scribe, I reckon, and never much at being a warrior. But if I keep up the boxing, maybe I'll be a good one in my next life."

"Are you still on that? If I've got to go around again, I don't want to always have TB," she said, tossing a hull at Conall.

He caught it and began twisting the long puckered shell. "No, no, that wouldn't be it. You'll be connected to the same people but maybe work out the mistakes you made in the last life."

"Who says I've made any mistakes?"

"All right, then, you'll just repeat them."

"Next time I'm young, I'll be sure to marry the rich suitor instead of the itchy-footed one," she joked.

"Oh, it wouldn't matter. Barbarians would have laid the rich man low eventually."

Maeve scooped the peas with her hand and let them slip through her fingers as she checked for spots. The peas pinged against the side of the wide metal bowl.

"Next time I'm young," she repeated. "'When I was young?—Ah, woeful When! / Ah! For the change 'twixt Now and Then! / This breathing house not built with hands, / This body that does me grievous wrong, / O'er aery cliffs and glittering sands, / How lightly then it flashed along.'"

"Whose poem was that?"

"Coleridge. I memorized that one when I was a girl, but I never really knew what it meant, not even when my mother died. 'Life went a-maying / With Nature, Hope, and Poesy, / When I was young!'"

"It's pretty, but I can't say that my young life has ever gone a-maying, though I like climbing the Caddo Peaks and reading and writing poetry, and have some hopes," Conall said.

"May Day comes only once a year." Maeve got up to pour the peas into a heavy pot and fetch a hambone from the icebox.

"Maybe human beings get one perfect moment, a minute or an hour, in a whole lifetime. A beam of sunshine glittering on an ancient Chinese urn packed with priceless ointment. The climb to a glacier that churns out water the color of emeralds and aquamarine. An hour spent slashing a sword next to Caratacus, knee-deep in blood. What would yours be?"

She sat back down and began peeling a red onion. "What would mine be? Don't let me forget to save the skins, because I'll boil them with some eggs."

"Sure," he said, looking out the window to where Caradog was chasing one of the cats from the feed shed. Somewhere close by a rooster was expanding his lungs and rehearsing how to drag a blistering Texas dawn over the horizon.

"It wouldn't be a perfect moment from here," she said. "I don't find this town much of a memory book. Your father just loves to tell tall tales and whoppers and chew the gossip with the locals, but I never have cared to join such spectacles. He knows how to fit right in with these country people who've never known anything better."

"He's a real sure-enough Texan," Conall murmured, still watching Caradog, who now was barking outside the shed.

"Each to his own," she said. She smiled, but her son did not see, his head still bent toward the dog.

"So what would your moment be?" The prodding was soft but tenacious, though he asked the question without turning to look at her.

"Maybe when I held my baby boy for the first time and saw how pretty and perfect he was?"

"Mama, you're not supposed to pick memories like that!"

"I don't know why not," she said firmly.

"Something else, then."

"How about when you were a little boy and gave me a valentine that promised to take care of me forever? Do you remember that? You looked so earnest, nodding your head, with your eyes all wide and serious."

"No, I meant something that's like a story or a poem," Conall said, shifting in his chair.

"Now don't get irritated."

"I'm not irritated," he said loudly.

Summer's hot wind off the plains blew in through the window, stirring his hair, drying the dampness on his back. They would be eating supper late, once the twilight brought a touch of coolness. Though the day was not humid, the air sapped Maeve's strength.

"Oh, maybe it was a May Day," she said. "I do remember a pretty May Day. I had been feeling weak all through April, and some traveling doctor examined me and told my stepmother that I had tuberculosis. That's Alice, your step-grandmother. She made me the loveliest dress from white lawn for a surprise. It was lined except for the sleeves and had embroidery and pin-tucks and lace—just homemade tatting, but sweet—and a ruffled collar that could be tied on to change the appearance. I don't know, but maybe she wanted to make something up to me. It wasn't long after we moved to Missouri, so I was feeling unsettled and missed my older brothers and sisters. That's when I changed my name. My mother had never given me a middle name—imagine!—so I added one and told everybody I wanted to be called *Maeve*, and my stepmother embroidered the name on the collar of my new dress. I wore it on May Day because I had been asked to a fancy party."

She reached up, touching her neck as if she could still feel the delicate fabric.

"April had been cold until near the end of the month, but May Day was perfect, mild and sunny. The party took place at a big stone house with a walled garden in the back. There must have been an orchard, because I remember a lot of trees in bloom—young fruit trees foamy with blossoms. Underfoot was grass, only somebody had taken a scythe and mowed it close, so neatly that the ground looked like a fancy carpet. As if they were lit from inside, the trees were luminous, and everybody told me that I looked like a flower, pale as snow. They were all very kind. I suppose they knew about my illness. People in coats and spring dresses stood around the edge of the garden while a gentleman sang one song in French and another in German. A lady recited poems—Herrick, I think it was—while the girls held hands in a ring around her. I felt very happy carrying my basket of buds and blooms, as though I were a bride, and then, to my everlasting surprise, I was picked as Queen of the May. They gave me a wreath of flowers and a scepter made out of an ash wand, with a bunch of apple blossoms tied on with ribbons, and I drove around the garden in a little cart hitched to a pair of goats with love knots on their harnesses."

She sighed heavily.

"How come you never told that story before? And you were a queen, too." Conall inspected his mother, his head tipped to one side.

"Queen Maeve of the May. I'd forgotten most of that until I started talking, and then it came back to me in a rush, the light in the trees and the cart and the young man singing. He must have been a foreigner. He had beautiful boots, wonderfully shiny, and a goatee."

"Goats and a goatee, too. That sounds a bit comical. And patent leather boots with a goatee? Bound to be a damn foreigner," Conall said.

Their eyes met, and mother and son broke into laughter.

"Nothing ever happens here," Maeve said, wiping her eyes.

"Chimney fires that burn down the house. Disaster on the derrick. The occasional murderous attack. Drunken harlots in the calaboose. Chickens running amuck on the banks of Turkey Creek. No, nothing much."

"Nothing exciting and wonderful," she amended. "Nothing beauteous and romantic."

"That's what drives me to box with Fletcher and to dream up yarns," Conall said. "Maybe if life meant art and heroes, I wouldn't even bother."

"What's your perfect moment? You were pestering me, and here you haven't told one."

"Oh, I was probably looking the other way and missed it. Or it's something marvelous that happened when I was too young to remember clearly, like when the star—that meteor—exploded and banged into the earth when we were staying by Crystal City."

"You can recall that, can you?"

"I guess so. Or else I heard the story so often that it made a story in my memory. In that case, maybe it was my first tale ever. The white fire streaking down the sky—I remember it. And I remember somebody taking me to see the meteorite. It looked to be about the size of a barrel and had ripped a trench into the ground."

Maeve got up, holding on to the chair, and set the dish on the table. "My hands stink of onions," she said, going slowly to the sink and scrubbing them, shaking her head when she sniffed at them once again.

Conall went on talking, half to himself.

"Maybe it was a face I caught sight of, down in New Orleans, with blue tattoos slashed across the cheekbone. Maybe a name chiseled on the door of a tomb. Maybe a secret."

Caradog was bothering the chickens now. They scuttled away from him, gargling in ruffled indignation.

Going to the door, Conall called into the yard. "Caradog! Hey, Cara—cut it out! Come on!"

The dog flashed across the expanse and leaped up. Settling at his master's feet, Caradog quivered as if he might jump again. Conall bent to pet him along the jaw and stroke his ears before opening wide the screen door.

"You always look like you're chuckling, even in this decrepit world of maniacs and cannibals," he told the dog. "What've you got to be cheerful about, you prankster? Playing tricks on the hens? You'd smile if you were playing with a rattler, wouldn't you? You watch out, now."

"He's one happy fellow," Maeve said.

"Sure is. I'll be back in a minute, Mama. Caradog and I have a little work to do."

At this, the dog grinned some more and followed him to the porch bedroom, toenails clattering on the floor.

Conall slipped inside. "I had an idea for a poem, Cara," he whispered. "You lie down and wait for me."

Obediently the dog flopped onto the floor.

Conall shoved his hand into his pants pocket, pulling out a quartz crystal. He palmed the stone for a moment, holding it tightly in his fist before letting it drop and reaching again into the pocket. This time he retrieved a coin, pausing to examine it before tossing it onto the bed beside the crystal.

Taking up a cheap drugstore tablet, he began to write.

Marly Youmans   101

Low Cotton

"Ain't you Doc's boy?"

The sharecropper had been puzzled about why the doctor's son wanted to pull cotton. "Why ain't you studying on delivering babies and fixing bones like your daddy?"

I'm a writer.

The sheer absurdity of the thought kept him from making any reply.

"Root of evil," Conall muttered, dragging the croker sack behind him. His fingers would be too sore to type by the time he could go home. He was sick to death of the hard bolls and the cudgeling of snakes and the labor of pulling cotton, sick of the bending that seemed an emblem of his troubles—bowing down to somebody else's demands, taking one menial job after another that sapped his strength and made him rage at the men who worked him rough and paid a pittance. At seventeen he felt brutalized and old. He'd tried a day at the gin and hadn't liked it much, had dabbled with a series of pick-up jobs. The farmer here hadn't hired enough field hands, though he was wild to get the crop in. Pickers were scattered across the landscape, each one with a world of cotton to harvest. The homemade straw hats of the farmer's own little boy and girls bobbed above the high cotton.

Noticing that the man's back was turned as he shouted to the woman on the porch, Conall straightened up and stretched. Heat was dancing on the cotton bolls at the foot of the field, rumpling the fabric of air.

"Could be a pirate ship floating on the water, about to hove into view," Conall whispered, and longed for a drink from the dipper and pail. The long thirsty gulp he had just taken seemed to recede into the previous week.

"Could climb on board and go ripping out of here to a place where there are no jobs, and everybody wants to hear a story," he told the cotton bolls. "I bet pirates love to hear a good tale."

When the farmer hollered at him to get back to work, Conall bent his aching spine to the cotton, remembering how sweet it had been to live in an out-of-town boardinghouse for the last of high school. Fletcher and other boys he knew had gone there as well, because the Cross Plains school stopped after tenth grade. The freedom of it! Though his mother had insisted on chaperoning him, he had found much to like about the new setting—a bookstore, friends who liked to write, local outlets and awards for his poems and stories and essays. He loved to lie on the cool wooden floor with his friends in the afternoons, drawing and telling stories or reciting poems until his mother came faltering through the door, looking tired and ill. In those moments of freedom before she returned from the daily errands, he could see the life he dreamed of glimmering ahead of him like the uncertain shine of a will-o'-the-wisp. But now the group was broken up, and the others had set about finding a man's work. Only he stubbornly refused advice. He would labor at anything, but he would not try to find meaning in it. He would make his own weird trail through the rattlesnakes and the sand roughs. Nothing in this town would he claim as a thing to be.

"The post office sure is a nice spot to work," one of his former teachers had suggested, "and they're hunting for somebody smart down at the drugstore. Somehow I thought you'd make a college boy and take over the practice from Dr. Weaver." Conall had nodded and been polite, "Yes, ma'am," but anger seamed him head to foot, as surely as a thunderbolt would scald and scar a post oak. None of them knew him. Oh, he might sort mail and sell stamps at the post office yet or mix sodas at the drugstore, but this misbegotten town would never lay claim to his soul. He had imagined that his townspeople might understand when he won gold and silver medals for his writing at school. But that was not real life to them, and now all creation was to be put away and a man's business taken up. The cumulus of dreams and tales that obliterated the sky, the storm clouds that darkened his imagination: these were classed as children's games, no better than playing with Caradog in the rocks and mesquite, pretending they were cave dwellers or pirates or Roman soldiers.

No, he determined. He would be a writer, no matter how foreign and wild it seemed to the locals, and nothing else would seize him for long—not college, not a vocation, not a father who fancied that his son might yet tote a doctor's bag and sew up the rambunctious fellows who fought at the icehouse or outside the dance hall. The local boom might have ended, but a few cowboys and oilmen hung around, enough for a fight and a few stitches.

"How can I write a story as big as Texas, if mighty Texas keeps treating me so mean?"

Tugging cotton free from the boll, he moved on, pushing the hat back from his soaked forehead. A slender Swainson's hawk screamed *kweeaaaaah!* in the unending blue of the sky, sailing straight into the bonfire of sun. Conall winced, looking up.

"Yeah, something as big as Texas," he murmured, "massive and heated and starry."

The White Horse

"You haven't told a story in a long time," Fletcher said. "Not even last month, when all the boys got together again, like we were in school."

"I haven't felt like a yarn in a pretty big stretch of time," Conall told him. "This whole damn town doesn't care about hearing anything from me except that I'm making money in one of its usual damnable soul-killer ways and therefore being what passes for an upright citizen."

A cold wind was blowing out of the northeast, bowling a few yellow leaves over the bare ground. The two friends walked along the edge of the road, occasionally kicking a stone into a field of winter wheat.

"Come on. Tell one. Even Caradog wants to hear a story. Look at that face—Cara is begging for one."

Conall leaned to let his hand slide along the dog's jaw and neck. "If people were all as nice as Caradog, what a sweet old world it would be."

"That's for sure—and my friend would be sure to wind me up a yarn whenever I asked." Fletcher winked at the dog.

"All right, I'll tell you a story. I heard or read something like this one a long time ago. Once there was a Mongol boy, a nomadic herder of sheep, who was presented with a gift, a lovely white horse, with pearly flanks and—what is more wonderful—wings of a perfect white. The creature simply appeared among the sheep one day, grazing on new grass, but he seemed to know the boy and followed him around like a dog and even knelt to let him mount. Many people were jealous of this good fortune, especially since the horse wore a silver collar set with sapphires and opals. When asked, the shepherd could not explain why Heaven had shown him such favor. He confessed that he had done nothing to deserve or request such an honor and joy."

Conall picked up a stick and tossed it for Caradog, who barked once and dived into the ditch at field's edge.

"In the morning he would thank the blue eternal Heaven for his horse and for a certain young girl beyond the mountain and river. She was the one promised to him when he was a child of six. He was sixteen now, a few years past the marriageable age, and soon he would be a husband. Often he idled away the hours in the pasture by making songs about love or about flying on the white horse. At noon, he would thank the blue eternal Heaven again, and then eat a meal of yogurt and dried meat. Tied to his sash next to a tinderbox, he had a little case engraved with a horse's head that held knife and chopsticks. When evening came, he would entrust the flock to his dearest friend and fly away over the mountain."

"Good Cara," Fletcher murmured, stooping to take the stick. Conall paused, reaching to stroke the dog's side.

"The white horse bore him up swiftly until the circular gers of his people looked like beads scattered far apart in the grass. It seemed that he could run a silk thread through the fire hole of each and string them around a neck! No, that wasn't possible. But perhaps blue eternal Heaven could do such a mighty thing. He felt so uplifted that, riding the white horse, he could see the souls shining in all things— the rocks and rivers, marmots and foxes, trees and wells. At the summit of the mountain towered a mighty larch. Each night the winged horse spiraled around the tree and then flew on, its wings glowing in the starlight. Never had the boy been so happy. He felt that the whole world was alive because of his love for the white horse and the girl on the other side of the mountain. Each evening when he landed in the field beside her house, the family would come out to welcome him, and he and the girl would walk in the wildflowers, the white horse grazing close beside them. They talked about the day when they would be married and the two of them would fly away together."

Conall picked up a rock and lobbed it far down the road. Caradog took off running, barking at the stone as it bounced.

"One night his friend was unable to watch the flock. Sadly the shepherd sat among his sheep, playing a flute. A scream of an animal in pain brought him to his feet—the image of a great cat attacking his beautiful white horse sprang into his mind. When he rushed to the field where the white creature liked to feed on grass or stand dreaming in the flowers, it was gone. Blood dabbled the flowers. The shepherd boy feared that spurs had been used on the tender flesh. He sat down and wept, but the flying horse did not come back. Neither did his friend reappear the next day.

"He left the sheep with his mother, asking her to care for them until he returned. It took him three days to reach his sweetheart's home. He slept in a tree each night, fearing wild animals. But when he reached her family's ger, the parents implored blue eternal Heaven for aid. His sweetheart was gone, stolen by his best friend, and no one knew the way to go. The shepherd was a nomad and not afraid to travel. He walked for seven days, staying in strange gers, trusting in the hospitality of strangers, asking about his horse and his beloved. On the seventh day he met a shaman who had seen the horse flying just above the treetops on a mountain slope."

Caradog had made a sweep through the field and was now back, jumping up on the boys, asking for another stick to be thrown. Fletcher snatched up a branch and flung it behind them. Conall turned to watch the dog leap into the air and catch the branch in his mouth before he went on.

"When he arrived at the place, he found the horse dying, the wings severed and abandoned close by, stained with black gore. The silver collar studded with jewels was gone. Burning with grief, the Mongol boy held the white head in his lap. With a last shudder, the horse passed from life, and its souls fluttered away. One perched on the world tree. Another came to him in a dream in the form of a ghost and told him to skin the body and take the bones. It was forbidden to eat the flesh because the winged horse was a noble being like the snow leopard or the *amur*, the Siberian tiger. The ghost gave him careful instructions on what was to be done.

"The next day the boy skinned the body and took the bones. He gave the flesh a wind burial because the horse was more of the air than of earth. Afterwards he made a sound box and covered it with horsehide, leaving a small opening in the back. He added a neck of horse bones, two strings made from exactly 235 hairs from the horse's tail, and a scroll carved into the shape of the horse's head. Then he traveled to the mountain tree that the white horse had loved. There he made a bow strung with horsehair and coated it with larch resin. When he had completed the instrument, he returned to the home of his lost bride and played for her parents. Sometimes they heard the wind blowing through the fields of the world and across the seas, and sometimes they heard the wild sounds of the horse calling for its master from the world tree."

Conall stopped, looking around for his dog before continuing.

"People named his instrument the *morin khuur*, or *fiddle-with-a-horse's-head*, and many more of them were constructed. In honor of the first maker, the two strings on later fiddles were called male and female, and one was made with hair from a stallion, the other from a mare.

"He never found his beloved wife-to-be, though he walked the length and breadth of Mongolia, playing his morin khuur. When the people asked him what he heard when he played, he said that the music was really the sound made by the now-invisible wings of the white horse. It wasn't simply that he heard the beating wings when the wind rushed past his ears, though that was also true. The music flew and bore him up, as the white horse had done. Sometimes when playing, he heard a bird singing in its throat—far off, on a branch of the world tree—or the voice of his lost bride, whispering at his ear."

In the silence after the close, Fletcher picked up a palm-sized rock and flung it high over the dirt road. The landing made a far-off clatter on pebbles and hardpan.

"That was a perfectly good story," he said, "but it wasn't one of yours. Not altogether."

Conall stood watching Caradog, who was now following a scent in a nearby field.

"No," he said. "I borrowed it. What I've learned is that I'm strong. It would take a lot to kill me. But these Cross Plains jobs eat me alive. I'm too damn weary to make up a story. I can't even imagine what sweet nothings the girl was singing in the shepherd's ear. Maybe I'm all washed up, pal."

"You're just getting started," Fletcher said. "You'll roam the world, telling tales. Like the boy in the story."

"Maybe so," Conall said. "Or maybe I'm like a meteor that burned up before it could fall to the earth."

Spoiled Flowers

A pair of wringer washers teetered on small feet, their one-arm handles flung up. Nearby, Conall lifted a red silk dress trimmed with handmade lace from a pail of soapy water. Each morning he made the rounds for the tailor's shop, collecting dirty laundry. By eleven, he was scrubbing at a washboard, and afterward he would make the deliveries of clean, ironed clothes. He didn't mind being out in the sun and air, mulling over episodes in a story or dreaming about ancient history, but he minded the grime of the dresses and undergarments.

That morning on his rounds, one of the local ladies of the night had demanded that he come inside a cramped room that stank of perfume and vomit and last night's trysts. He stood by the tumbled, blowsy bedclothes, glancing at the sheets and then away. Perhaps his knock had roused her from bed, for her yellow hair was uncombed, and she wore a sky-blue, wine-stained bathrobe, tightly cinched. Once more he felt a loathing for the boom that had made this little town into the haunt of roughnecks and harlots. He hated it, the whole so-called *civilization* with its brazen excess and its cravings for money and violence. No peace, balanced between times of luxury and times of barbarism, could last long and perhaps only existed in stray moments, he concluded.

Not for the first time, he thought about lighting out for distant shores. Staring at the cracked wall as though at a map of boundaries and rivers, he conjured the boats he had seen as a child at the port of New Orleans. He could take a ship to Dublin and discover for himself the emerald grasses and the trickles of water that splashed into the peat cuttings. It would be something fine to see a menhir in mist and little islands where anchorite monks had clung to the rocks like oysters—mortifying their flesh for the sake of a pearl of great price. He wanted to see Scotland and go on walks where the blue-tattooed Picts used to dodge and feint, hiding from enemies.

The whore gave him a dollar for his trouble after she had bundled the dresses, spotted and ring-straked with vomit and moonshine, and shoved them into his arms.

"That's A-e—wait—A-e-m-e-l-l-e-a. Aemellea Meringue Beauregard. *Miz* Beauregard. Got it? Do what you can," she ordered, pinching his cheek. "I'm going home soon, and I need my gowns in order. Tell the tailor to repair the things any way he can, and I'll pay." She tapped her foot in emphasis, exposing a slipper and silver pompom.

"All right," he said, putting a hand to his face where the touch of her fingers still burned.

"Oh, damn it to hell," she said.

"Is this all? Is there something else?"

"My best man did me wrong," she said plaintively, looking abruptly young and vulnerable.

Conall wondered if Aemellea Meringue Beauregard had gotten the phrase out of the pulp pages of *Adventure* or from some woman's magazine of true confessions, though perhaps the sentiment fit. Probably she couldn't read and didn't care whether she ever learned. But she'd heard about such things—maybe she picked up the cliché from the other whores. Was it a Mr. Beauregard she meant or somebody else?

"I'm sorry," he said.

"Sometimes love is the same thing as hate."

This, too, sounded like some trite wisdom she had borrowed from a magazine, though the words made him feel uneasy.

"Maybe so," he said.

"I reckon hate can hold you just as close as love," she added, with a note of surprise in her voice that suggested she had just now thought of that one.

"I guess."

"You're so sweet," she said, and at the words, tears formed as if by magic on her eyelashes. She pulled another coin from a little purse tucked into her cleavage and gave it to him, kissing him on the cheek.

At that he had blushed, slipped the coin into his pocket, and left the place before one of her sweeping, cloud-like moods could turn again. Soon she might stamp her foot in those low green heels with the silver pompoms on the toe, and shout, "Why on earth did I give good money to the tailor's boy!" Once out of sight, he scrubbed at his cheek with a handkerchief, as if the spot might be touched by disease. Thanks to garrulous Doc Weaver, Conall knew all about how the clap had boiled through the oilmen and shopkeepers who frequented whores drawn to town by the boom.

The red dress was from Aemellea Beauregard's wardrobe, and he'd tried every solution in the row of bottles to remove the stains. He figured that the two coins meant he had to try, but now he was fixing to give up.

The tailor poked his head out the door of the shop, checking on the wash.

"I can't do any more for this one," Conall called, and with clothespins clipped it next to a yellow dress trimmed with limp green lace. He pointed to dark spatters that might have been wine, might have been blood.

"Maybe I can stitch in a new bodice from white silk after it dries. She's a generous, accommodating sort of young lady, if a little stained." The tailor winked at him. With a wave, he went back inside. Through a window, Conall could glimpse him measuring some trifling fellow for a new suit.

The hems of the wet gowns fluttered in the breeze, and the drier ones lifted as if to sail on the wind before sinking back down. Without their owners, they smelled of soap and fresh air and were free to frisk in the sunshine. But every week lately, fewer dresses frolicked on the line—the oil fever caught contagion elsewhere, and what was left of the local boom ebbed.

In the late afternoon he walked home, delivering a few final packages on the way. From the steps he could hear his mother and father arguing, so he made a show of opening and shutting the front door, and then went into the back yard with Caradog. He played with the dog for a while, tossing a ball, and let him inside the house for a treat. His mother was planted in her usual spot, while his father stood opposite, arm on the top rail of a rocking chair. Conall noticed that Maeve looked a little paler than usual.

"Your father was just leaving," she said quietly.

"I don't know," Doc said. "I might stay put a while, though I've got a farm lady to see to yet. Real good cook, too. Now there's a woman who knows how to feed a man who's been working hard. She'll have thought to save a plate of food for me."

"We wouldn't want to keep you from a patient."

"Your ma's nerves are not feeling any too well today, son." Doc winked at Conall. "Did I tell you about the hog and the harlot who met on the train trestle?"

The boy laughed. "Yes, sir. That was a grade-A joke."

"It sounds like the sort of country jest that's not fit to tell a child," Maeve said, subsiding into the depths of the couch.

"A child? He's scrubbing the business out of the whores' damn dresses and underthings every blessed day," Doc roared.

Maeve lifted her chin and looked at her husband. He plucked up an almanac and began to peruse it closely, all the time whistling a passage from a song that began, "I sent my wife to the Thousand Isles."

The room was simple, with only a couch and chairs and a rocker that somebody had dragged in the last time visitors came. A few tables served to hold a book or two and a velvet bouquet under a dusty glass. The bunch of flowers had been purple with bright persimmon stamens when "Eddie and Maevie" had received it as a wedding present. Over the years the Texas sun had faded the original colors to an unattractive dark mauve and pink, and finally to brown. A number of times one or the other had threatened to throw it away, but somehow nobody had. Whenever either of them noticed it, the ailing curio was said to possess a certain fascination in transformation and decay. Otherwise, the chamber appeared wholly unremarkable and showed little trace of an attempt to make the sitting area cheerful and attractive.

Conall edged out of the room and headed to the kitchen, where he ate a dish of cold chicken that he found in the icebox, sharing the stringy breast meat with Caradog. Afterward, he pored through his papers and books, planning what he would do next with a story. He wanted the course of it to run headlong from start to finish, like a cataract that starts somewhere high—way up in the heavens, maybe—and plunges straight to mountain peaks and jolts downward for miles before crashing with a frenzy of foam into a bottomless lake where nameless creatures stir.

Fletcher was home for a visit and wanted to see him in the evening. If nothing got in his way, they could go out.

He paused, wondering if he had heard a shot. No, there was his mother, calling to him, her voice strained. Doc must have banged the door shut when he went out again. Bleak and small, Maeve's cry seemed to hover in the stale air of the bedroom that was once a porch.

"Honey, do you think you could help me into bed?"

Big as All Texas

"How could I do a thing like that, Fletcher?"

"Your old man could be the answer. Why doesn't he help out more? She's got tuberculosis, and he's a doctor. I just don't understand why everything's on you, Conall. All this doesn't make sense the way it ought."

Fletcher reached down and rubbed Caradog behind the ears. With the dog curled on the trunk between them, the two young men were sitting in the canopy of a windfall tree that had made the mistake of setting its roots in sand. A pair of horses grazing near the road had carried them miles away from the electric lamps of home. Now twilight was conquering the blazing enormity of the Texas sky and Venus was appearing, along with a few attendant stars.

"He's busy. He's got patients all over the place. Half the time we don't see him at dinner or supper, and sometimes he goes tearing off before breakfast. I bring home money, but it doesn't much matter if I'm heaving freight or picking cotton or something else—none of it makes a difference to me. You know what's funny? City Drugstore is worse than writing the oil news or being a stenographer or any of the other damn things I've done in the past few years. Head soda jerk, nothing—just plain old jerk, that's me, with bastards to tell me what to do every second. The most fun I've had these past few years has been with those rough-necks who asked me to box at Neeb's icehouse."

Conall took a long pull of home brew, and Fletcher leaned forward, intent on reaching him.

"You remember when you sold your first story to *Weird Tales*? You got down on your knees by your bed and prayed, you were so glad."

"Yeah, that felt as big as all Texas," Conall said. "I can still catch a glimmer of that feeling, when I think about it hard. You know, I'm making just about enough money to quit my job, and that's what I'm going to do—nothing but write."

"Then why can't you go off on your own, work hard and sell more stories—come home to visit your parents the way other people do? Maybe you'd find some more reasons to get down on your knees. Maybe they'd be glad, too, when you showed what you could do with a little independence." Fletcher grasped his friend's arm for a moment, shaking it lightly. "You're on a short leash, Con."

"It's rugged to explain a thing like this," Conall said. "I owe my mother so much because she's the one who encouraged me when nobody else did. But it's not just that I'm grateful. It's that she's so slight and helpless and sick. She's had a bitter life, what with one problem after another…she took care of her younger brothers and sisters when she was a girl, and after that she nursed the older ones who had TB, and then she got taken ill. It's been hard with my father always moving from one bugtussle Texas town to another, never lighting where she could take it easy—"

"How about hiring a woman to help out?" Fletcher's question didn't stop the rush of words.

"—and finally ending up here where the people don't like her so well, and some say she's too refined and above them because maybe she served them on fancy china at dinner when we first moved here or didn't care for country pranks and jokes. Her ancestors were kings

Maze of Blood

and queens in Ireland, so maybe she had a right to plates with a gold rim and to setting a fine table. Nobody notices that she's weaker all the time, but she is, and yet she just goes on being brave."

"Everybody's got troubles, Con, some more and some less, but your parents—don't you think it's wrong that they won't let you be free?" Fletcher gestured toward the distance. "All our friends from school are scattering and pulling down good jobs, even settling down with a steady girl. They're not bad about writing a letter, but that's going to peter out over time, and then you'll be even more alone. Your old man won't let you go because he doesn't want to take care of your mama, and your mama won't let go because she wants you to stay."

"That's just not so!" Conall toppled from his branch and landed in a pile of pin-oak leaves.

"You all right, pardner?" Fletcher bent down to see what was happening, and Caradog got to his feet, whining.

"I ought to march you over to the icehouse and box some sense into you, Fletcher!" Conall swayed. He handed over his beer before clambering back into the tree. "This is a cruel old world, and in times to come the U. S. of A. will be sliding downward into the black maggoty pit, a place where men dream only of money and sex instead of love and beauty, and religion falls apart, and war becomes a game. Some day barbarians will come battering at our gates, and bust on through to smash us like rock salt pounded in a mortar. And you go to blaming somebody who wants to help out and make one person's life a little better."

"Nah," Fletcher said. "I just thought it was worth a try. Don't you want a best girl? Don't you want to get married some day? This here old dog's not going to last forever." At this, Caradog stirred and perked up his ears.

"A girl ties a man down."

"Your mama—oh, never mind." Fletcher drained the mason jar of beer and looked around for the jug.

"It's the clash of civilizations, my friend. That's what's causing all the trouble here and everywhere. Like a cosmic boxing match, one world against another, each taking turns to be up or down, decadent or barbaric. Poor farmers hitting the oil jackpot and turning into drunks. Regular boys running after dope. Girls who sat at the next desk in third grade now wearing turquoise silk cut low over their breasts, advertising a fire sale. The town was young, but in the first boom month it grew long in the tooth, lax, and unclean. People ride a seesaw and are seldom in balance, and only for a moment. That's the whole truth."

"Conall, you brew a damn fine beer. There's another truth for you."

"I can't disagree with that one. And I make a mighty swell night with stars, if I do say so myself."

The two young men lay back in the fallen tree, staring up at the constellations that glittered from the low horizon to the zenith.

Conall waved his empty mason jar, as if to fill it with starshine. "You could take all the jewels of English kings and queens out of the Tower of London and fling them up in the sky, and it wouldn't be half so bodaciously pretty as the light from this bunch of burned-out gas balls."

Throne of Ice

Moonlight glimmered on the icehouse door and fell through the lock, casting a moon the size of a lucky penny on the floor. Conall listened to the musical seep from the drain for a moment before walking in. The boys were careless about leaving ajar the door to their perishable treasure.

Blue Northern ice mounted to the ceiling like a gigantic throne, its topmost slab glittering with more coins of moonlight, scattered from a roof vent. Close to the edges were blocks of wild ice that darkened to emerald but held blebs, sprigs of fir, the occasional leaf or cone still linked to a twig—even, once, a bewitching white flower. At the core was the best ice, a clear sapphire of pond ice that had been tended and swept clean until harvest.

For an instant he wanted to wander north of the star-shaped state that had governed his days—to see the men in their bright plaids from the great Yankee woolen mills as they urged the mule across with the snow scraper and ice plow, clearing and marking the surface for the hand saw and breaking bar, while a boy ran behind, cleaning the ice. Hook in hand, he'd walk a block along the channel cut in the ice, letting it bobble in the water as if he were guiding a woman along a dance floor. The cold would tell him that he wasn't in Texas anymore: he'd wrestle the ice onto the bobsled with tongs and drink whiskey from a flask shared with the other men, while children fished for broken hunks of ice with a net.

"Dreaming again? You are a dangerous man, Conall Weaver!" The voice was relaxed, amused. "So this is your castle of barbaric glass, is it? Where you batter your fists on your enemies?"

"Kaletor!"

"Yes. Kaletor of the Sapphire Throne is seated on a chair of ice smack in the center of the mighty pinwheel of Texas." The king laughed with pleasure and leaped onto the icehouse floor. "You have a strange palace."

"It's not mine—I just borrow it to box."

"Not yours? But it is a fitting place, all the same. And what ground can a man claim, even if he harries the Western isles and claims the Citadels of Splendor? Tell me."

"I claim nothing. I'm a fool."

Kaletor's eyes, the color of a sea running gray and cold, raked over him.

"Well said. I also am a fool."

"But a king."

"Boy of Heliki, king of Akhaïa...both are one, and a fool," he said, clapping Conall on the back so that he stumbled. "What is a palace but a thing like this room of ice, fit only to melt away with the years? I am only a straw in the wolfish wind that blows down houses. In the history of a city, I am a mote, lasting no longer than the blink of an eye. And even a proud capital's towers and temples will go down to dust, just as the mountain will shrink to a molehill and the valley be thrust up toward the stars."

"My heart's as pitted as an old cow bone in the Texas sun," Conall said. "I have done nothing, made nothing worth the keep. Shining and mysterious as I meant them to be, my packed words will melt just like a chunk of cold sky fallen from the rear of an ice wagon.

Nor have I roved away and been free. I've been so hobbled since childhood that I can hardly come or go."

"What matter?" King Kaletor let out a long kite-tail of laughter that buoyed Conall's mood.

"So is the goal to be high and unrepenting?"

He laughed again. "Hah! Perhaps I am worth my keep. Let's wrestle in your palace, Conall Weaver."

The aquamarine of the ice swam in the darkness, and when the wind blew, the little flakes and minnows of moonlight flittered. A breath off the Northern snows passed over the two men like the paranormal wake of a ghost.

"What will you give me if I do? You're a king, and I'm a joke."

"Hasn't a ruler ever been scorned? You gave me vinegar to drink often enough!" Kaletor threw his head back to laugh once again. "I'll give you the blessing of a king if you can pin me."

"All right," Conall said.

Kaletor the king stood in a beam of moonshine, looking as fearsome, as arrogant, and as innocent as an angel.

Seizing hold, he threw the Texan to the ground. Conall grappled with him, and though he knew that Kaletor was impossibly hard and strong, his hands passed through the flesh and the figure fell into handfuls of shadow and moonlight.

"Grip fast, Conall Weaver, and I will bless you—"

Conall's hands tightened into fists. He was alone with the waves of cold and shadows from the ice. And it was not his dream ice—the sawn harvest ice of earlier days with leaves and stems—but plain, identical blocks of manufactured ice.

Bleak and modern.

When he opened a hand like some coarse, homely flower, he found only the useless pollen of moonshine gilding his palm.

Death of a Dog

"Mama, do you remember that girl in the pink dress—the one knocked down by the runaway ice wagon and trampled under the wheels?"

Conall sat on the floor cross-legged, stroking the head of his dog. Caradog opened his eyes and gave a single twitch of an ear before sinking back into sleep.

"Oh, and that was a terrible time to be sure. I didn't know you would recall that day. Seems like a long time ago now," Maeve said. "They rushed her to the house, covered with blood and all white and crushed. The little colleen. A pretty half-Irish thing with rosy cheeks, she was. Her name was Clare-Elizabeth, and the Cooleys called her *Clare-Bitsy* instead of *Clare-Betsy* because she was so small. The poor mother set up a cry when they said the doctor wasn't at home. But then your father drove up, and all that big crowd parted like the Red Sea to let him come in. They'd already laid the little girl on the kitchen table. Some men were shouting that she had already passed on. Rose Cooley couldn't accept it, and she keened fit to wake the dead."

"But she had, hadn't she? Clare-Elizabeth, I mean. She was already dead, wasn't she? I don't like to think of it." Conall felt sure he remembered the little girl carried on a wide board, rushed into the kitchen.

A handful of tossed okra caps rang against the side of a tin bucket.

"Yes, Clare-Elizabeth had gone far beyond stirring, and I suppose it was for the best because the child's body was mangled. She would've been dreadfully crippled if she had lived. I'm sorry you have that memory."

Maeve wiped her hands with a dishrag. Okra seeds had stuck to her fingers, and she flicked them into the bowl.

"Your father gave the poor woman a draft of medicine that put her out for more than a day. I don't believe Rose was ever quite right in the head after Clare-Bitsy died. Somehow I managed to get to the funeral, though I wasn't so very well. The Cooleys moved away not long afterward, and the father had the body exhumed and taken with them, wherever it was they went, along with the marker. The grave-stone had a sleeping lamb on top and just the name *Bitsy* below. He did all that to satisfy his wife, I heard, because she couldn't bear to leave the girl alone, no one to visit the grave. But you just put that day out of your mind. It has been a long, long time since Clare-Bitsy passed on."

Conall sighed, taking one of the dog's paws in his hand.

"I'll be running down to Brownwood for a few days."

"Honey, go right ahead," Maeve said. "You go to the bookstore and the library and just do some work that you need to do, and come back when it's right."

He got up and went to his room, where he could be heard jerking open the ill-fitting drawers of his dresser.

Before leaving, he held Caradog close and let the dog lick his hand.

"Why can't a dog live for as long as a human? I'm an Iron Man in the ring," he said. "I can take all the punishment the boys down at the icehouse dish out. Right now I've got two black eyes to prove it. And I can put up with whatever else comes down the pike. But this, Cara, I can't bear."

During his days in Brownwood, Conall spent hours at the library or wandered the streets. He was alone a good deal. One day he sat down on a bench with an old-timer.

"Quite a pair of shiners you got there," the man said.

"Pretty right about now, aren't they? Just like a double rainbow. Got them boxing down at Neeb's icehouse in Cross Plains. Gave as good as I got, too."

"Looking at you, I was afeared that you got the seat of your britches kicked out. I used to love a good fight when I was a youngster. After a while, though, I'd racked up too many damn scalps and didn't love it no more. It got to be downright serious." The old man wheezed as he laughed and then reached in his pocket to offer some tobacco.

"No, thank you, sir," Conall said. "You from around here? I don't see buckskins so often nowadays."

"Might as well be here as anywhere," he said. "Grew up in Kentuck. When I was fourteen, I was on fire with stories about the wilderness. My blood was just crying out for the prairies and the mountains. We had a royal dunderhead of a dog that was always yapping after squirrels, and I wasn't much different. Seems I could smell the adventure blowing in from the west. Ever seen a cat cavorting and rolling in some bushy catnip? Well, I was that cat, and the West was my catnip plant."

He rubbed at the unshaven stubs along his jaw.

"Ma wouldn't have it. But those tales just made me seethe to get out, and it wasn't long before I plain boiled over and ran off on her. I'm not proud about that. But I nosed out plenty of adventure. I've crisscrossed the country on these feet many a time. Used to be a scout, leading wagon trains west from Missoura. It was exciting for a mere fool of a boy, and I got to know the different tribes and their cunning ways. Made some good friends, too. There's a lot of fascination to an Injun. I've fought more Sioux and Comanche than you have boxers, I bet."

"I'd like to hear about those skirmishes. You must be pretty well up there in years."

"If I'm not 99, I'm 98, or maybe 102. Let's just make it a round 100. Ain't that prodigious? Whoever heard of such a Methuselah age?"

"Yes, sir, that is something."

"But Injun fighting ain't much to talk about—killing is killing in the end, though saving your scalp and not ending up skinned and roasted over a Comanche fire is mighty motivating. What's a young fellow like you doing in this fair excuse for a city?"

"My dog took sick, and he's not going to make it, and so I just had to get out of town," Conall said.

The old man stared at him for a long moment. Once more he scraped a hand along the stubble of his jaw, making a dry, rasping sound. Then, with a quick nod of the head, he launched back into speech.

"I've had me some fine dogs in my day. And a few I wouldn't give a chawed quid to have back. The kind of imbeciles that would bark at a knot. But I had one that I liked the best, for all that he was just a mongrel like me. Saved my life more than once," the old man said, pausing to send a squirt of tobacco into the dry grass. "He had the finest nose west of the Mississippi: a more delicate instrument of nasal sensation there never was. Why, that old boy could smell a Comanche ten miles off! On point he was always just as calm and collected as a lady drinking China tea with her pinkie in the air. Having arrows skirring around and bullets ricocheting was just roast beef with gravy and popovers to him. He ate it up. I can remember him sticking as close as a tick during a buffalo stampede, with the prairie running wild and dangerous like a flash flood. Even then, the mutt stayed cooler than a man.

"It's my considered belief that there's only one woman, one cause, and one dog that comes along in a man's life. And a dog might be just as big as the other two."

"I'm with you there," Conall said. "What was his name?"

"I called him *Dog*. Or *Good Dog*. Because he sure was that. Occasionally I called him *You Jackass*, but that was all in fun. You know, he had his cravings just like a boy. He loved passenger pigeons better than any other food on earth. You don't see those birds anymore, and I reckon that's because of Dog. That animal was purely devastation on squab."

The man Conall had now secretly named *The Old Scout* fumbled in his pouch of tobacco, fingers trembling.

"Dog relished most any bird except heron. Once I was down in Virginie, and some damn fool of a nincompoop shot a blue heron and skinned it and cooked the breast. Why would you eat a bird that God Almighty made for nothing but looks? Made for the fun and the joy of it, I reckon. Them birds eat mud bugs and frogs, and I tell you, there's bound to be a flavor of marsh grass and periwinkles about a coastal heron. I could tell it wasn't going to be tasty, because Dog turned up his nose."

The old man's eyes moistened as he laughed.

"I sure did miss that dog. A poisoned arrow struck him in the gut—the only time I heard him give a whimper. He knew when I reached for the gun, and he just set his paw right on my hand as if to say he was with me on the need, and then he lay back easy and closed his eyes. I shot him underneath a wagon, with Injuns and settlers howling and screaming all around. Afterward, I carried him off and buried him secret-like, so nobody could dig him up and stew him. He was a dog of adventure, famous for spunk and gumption, and he deserved better."

"You did him proud," Conall said.

"I treated my dog better than I treated a lot of people, though I did get back to visit Ma before she died, and glad of it, too. She was a well-spoken woman, and she had pictured me being a schoolteacher. But when a boy gets called by something that wants to make him into a man, he's bound to follow."

Maze of Blood

The tale of Dog and one pioneer's part in the smash-up between two civilizations stirred Conall, and he wished he had some token of respect to give.

"You scouts did a great thing, opening the West."

"It was there."

Conall echoed the words, so plain and manly, accepting of the endless wheel of change and the tilting of one empire against another, barbarianism and civilization locked in an eternal struggle—and wasn't that a frontiersman's way, to take the thing because it was there to be taken?

The scout nodded. "Those stories about the territories, they were strong. Never be such tales to set boys alight again, not till we send mule-skinners to the stars. If we ever do. The West is all used up."

"Mule-skinners to the stars! I like that." Conall laughed, surprised at the fanciful thought.

Grasping an arm of the bench with both hands, the old man scooted forward. "Mighty nice talking to you, young fellow. My daughter's coming up the street, so I'll be loping off. I can tell the sound of that creakety, crickety old wagon."

Sure enough, a mule and wagon stopped close by. A woman who looked no more than thirty called a greeting, and the one-time scout hoisted himself up and tottered toward her. Straight black hair was pulled back and pinned up in a braided coil, and Conall wondered what tribe the mother had called her own. If her father really was a hundred years old, he must have been attractive to women when he was seventy. What strength, to go on without bowing to time!

In a few minutes, the pair was carried out of sight.

Conall walked slowly back to the house where he was staying and dialed the number for home. He turned toward the wall so that nobody who came in could see his face.

"Mama," he said, "How's Caradog?"

The Black Cat

It's funny how much difference a dog's death can make.

And it wasn't just that no four-legged pal came to greet Conall as he walked toward the house or accompanied him on rambles in the country—his friends so often away or busy now—or even that there was no companionable warmth settled on the end of his bed while he bent over the typewriter, gesturing and sometimes talking loudly as he dreamed up his stories. Unlike a few of the neighbors, the dog had never complained. Caradog had even leaped to his feet and barked with sheer joy at the exultant words. It wasn't even that nothing and nobody else in his life had loved him quite that way, with steadfastness and without making a single demand except that they race and jump and play together in the sun. In memory, the dog's love shone with a purity and stainlessness that prevented Conall from even considering another puppy.

The loss meant a great change in people.

No longer did they stop him to admire Caradog. No one exclaimed over the curious cross of collie and Walker hound. Nobody knelt to rub the dog's head and ears.

Now Conall walked by himself, and as he didn't care much about clothes and had grown burly by splitting firewood out back and boxing, he looked more like a roughneck than most of the men in the town. Children fell away from his life almost entirely, simply by the death of the dog. Mothers would clutch their little sons and daughters by the hand and turn away if they saw him hurrying along the street. Often enough a scrape reddened his cheek, or shiners painted his face in blues and yellows and reds. Young women no longer had a reason to say hello, and men mostly nodded, if that.

Conall was getting a reputation. He seemed a loiterer to solid men with jobs that had a starting time and ending time, and he ranted stories like a wild man—and anybody who wanted to be caught looking at the pulps down at the drugstore could see the Weaver name, printed alongside some picture that looked just decent enough to hide in the drawer of a bedside table, though Doc was prone to carrying a folded magazine under his arm to show his men friends.

In the evenings he liked to drink beer at Neeb's and box with what was left of the oilmen. The landscape around town had changed, many of the derricks remaining but the spudders and Star machines hauled away to the next hamlet that was slated to suffer an explosion of harlots and roughnecks and petty gangsters. Conall barely noticed. He wasn't working downtown any longer. Though he had made some sales, he felt under pressure to produce more stories, to make so much money that it would explain and justify and demand his staying home in the porch room, hammering at the type-writer, crafting the sentences that made neighbors think a writer was a mad creature to have around. Thus, son and mother spent a great deal of time indoors in their own world, he writing for hours on end and she sleeping or waking to fix him something to eat, if she felt well enough. Maeve stayed at home so much that she hardly knew the boom was over.

For Conall, the trip to the post office became much more impor-tant—keeping track of the friends from school who had vanished into the Texas landscape was vital to him, though the notes grew shorter and less frequent.

When the letter from Wildsmith came, he felt a great joy spiraling through him, and that afternoon he went horseback riding until he felt lost, and then he took out the sheet of paper and read the words over again. At last he had touched somebody who mattered to him, out there beyond the walls of the town.

The borrowed horse nibbled at the paper. Conall laughed and pulled the treasure away, folding the sheet up and placing the envelope in the pocket over his heart.

"I wish feelings could be bottled," he said, stroking the horse's mane. "It's a pity, but all the bad stuff burns deep in your memory, and the good just blows away like tumbleweeds and ashes."

At home, they had been wondering where he had gone.

"I got a letter from Phillip Wildsmith," he told them.

"Oh, that's really nice, isn't it?" Maeve's voice wavered, sounding tired or uncertain.

"The writer," he said.

He glanced at his mother and then looked away. The dilapidated couch seemed to be devouring her. The place where she habitually sat each afternoon looked sunken and soiled, although perhaps that was only shadow. Conall rubbed a hand over his eyes, as if to clear his sight. Her face was unusually drained of color today, with two hectic spots. The image stayed in his mind—the white, with flecks of red, the rotting sofa—and he thought how strange it was, when he so rarely noticed anything about the house. Maybe he was seeing it the way Wildsmith would see, he thought. Maybe that was why he saw it anew, grotesque and blighted.

"This Wildsmith fellow, he's important?" Doc Weaver stared at his son over the tops of his glasses.

"He's great," Conall said. "He says a lot of other writers in his circle like my yarns, too."

The words sounded like a lie to his ears. He knew none of his news meant anything, not really, to either one of them, at least not in the way he longed for it to mean to somebody. His mother would be pleased for him, and his father would be brooding over whether this new link to a famous writer meant something useful—that is, if it would mean money. Conall wondered what friend he could surprise with the news, but there didn't seem to be anyone at all. To think of the whole population of a town, and not one person to tell! But he would send notes to his friends from school. Some of them were still trying to write. They would recognize the name and be glad for him, though it wasn't the same as telling somebody who cared face to face. He wished Fletcher was home.

He couldn't even tell his dog! When he came home after Caradog's death, the back lot had been harrowed end to end. His parents had tried to erase any evidence of a grave.

He went into the porch bedroom and sat down to read the letter again, but he had lost his pleasure in the thing.

"More of them will come," he muttered.

Why had he been condemned to this hole? Hardly one person in town would read a poem for pleasure, or pick up a book. Nobody but his former teachers, and he had hated the local school with such passion that he didn't want to see any of their faces. Once he had attended a luncheon to talk about writing, but he couldn't bear the pink tablecloth and the little ruffled cups with the candies inside. The stiff faces of the ladies told him that he wasn't what they had meant at all in asking for a writer, not even in his good brown suit. He had begun to sweat profusely, and by the time he got out of there, his shirt was drenched.

"Damn." He flinched at the memory of what he had said—a jumble of blue tattoos, exploding civilizations, barbarian hatchets, and girls.

After a while he slipped out of the house, first telling his mother that he'd be back in time to help her get ready for bed. Doc had gone off on a case, it seemed. He was gone, at any rate. Conall hurried over to the icehouse, but the boys had melted away. The room was empty of all but a few blocks of ice, the smell of sweat almost tangible. Didn't they know he was coming? He should have set a time to spar.

Only a small fastidious mouser was in residence, oblivious to him while licking a paw. He fetched a few beers from the boxers' private cache, leaving an IOU in payment, and plunked himself down in a protesting straight chair to drink.

"Cat," he said, "I got a letter from Phillip Wildsmith."

She paused in her washing.

"I see you know the name. All the black cats know, I suppose. Pretty soon I'll be hearing from lots of writers. Bound to happen. Sounds pretty thrilling, doesn't it?"

The little black cat ambled over to him, rubbing against his leg, and he reached down to pet her.

"I don't normally have much truck with cats," he said, starting on a second bottle. "A transaction with a cat is fraught with danger, you see. There's a reason that the old Arabic and Persian chroniclers say that Genghis Khan had cat's eyes. Green is what they were, the color of magic and danger. A cat's just not like a dog. A dog will save your neck and your poor old mama's, too, but a cat will let you hang. It will sit and watch and even take a bath while the whole consarned town marches in with burning crosses and a rope and strings you up from the chandelier. If you've got a chandelier, which I don't. But I believe they might string me up anyway, given the chance. Might even put in a chandelier just to hang me."

He nodded at the thought of a chandelier in the icehouse.

"Yep. Or maybe they'd tar and feather weird old Conall. That's why I come here and box, see. Can't let the locals get ahead of me. Or maybe it's because I might try to string somebody else up, if I didn't work it out by pummeling two eyes and a nose and a mouth."

The cat looked at him steadily, seeming neither to agree nor disagree, but then she hopped into his lap and curled up.

"Ouch! You got quite the claws, missy. You don't give a damn about my thigh, do you? I bet you're blazing hell on rats." He petted her, but the fur was as coarse and dry as any barn mouser's. Still, she began to purr as he stroked her under the chin.

"Don't think you're doing me any favor with that racket. If you're not biting a rat in the neck, you aren't helping me out. You know, puss, I've lived all over Texas, and I've seldom had call to be grateful to cats."

He swigged from the bottle.

"Back east, I'll bet the ladies always have cats, and not just to keep the mice down. I suspect they're a bunch of fancy cat-worshippers. I'll bet they spend hours with those cats on ancient velvet cushions in their laps, combing and combing the fleas and ticks and assorted insect vermin out of their long tangled fur. The mice go to scrabbling, and the cats swoop down and hiss and pounce or else lie in wait, silent as two or three dozen graves. But all that ruckus is nothing compared to our old house, back when I was glad to have a cat around."

Conall stroked the cat under her chin and along the jaw.

"We had a dear infant who came by to pay a visit, and a rat came along and nibbled the infant's toes. The young mama, who thought they were darling little pink peas, shrieked until she was forced to sit down with a very hot toddy and her feet in a pan of Epsom Salts. I never did know what good the salts did, but the soaking kept her from running about screaming for a while. Those rats had chewed a hole in the bedroom wall and came swarming in. I guess they caught the scent of a sweet baby and thought they'd have that morsel of apple dumpling for supper. My mother chunked a rock at the leader and hit him square on the nose, but it wasn't any good. The old Ratsputin just stood up on his hind legs and jeered at her. He called my mama rude names—rattish ones like *bandicoot* and *flophouse doe* and *fleabag*—until she had to go take a lie-down with a lavender-sprinkled handkerchief on her brow.

"This is all true, mind," he said.

The cat blinked sleepily and shut one eye.

"Another notable cat-event in our family happened when some rats ganged together and dragged a squawking hen off her nest in the chicken house. It was a good box nest, too, well made and comfortable with the best grade-A straw, but they slung the chicken on the floor and crunched into those precious eggs. Carried the durn things off wholesale and flogged them down in the nether bowels of Rat City. Probably made a mint of money, too. They bit a guinea hen in the neck and sucked her dry, tore the flesh from her skinny bones. The henhouse was a pure shambles. Our rooster—always a temperamental boy—keeled over in a faint and was bagged by the rats and never spied again, except for two tail feathers, one rusty and one deep green-black, left like calling cards on the henhouse floor. My mother wore the pair for years on her best hat, in memory of the cowardly cock.

"The place smelled rank. Rat pee in the cupboards. Fat black rice grains in the meal bin. Squeaks and rat-shrieks in the walls, so loud they rattled the lathe and made the plaster fall."

Conall took another drink.

"So listen up. We imported a cat from the next farm—a feline of generous proportions and considerable fame in that part of Texas, with teeth like rapiers and claws like sharpened dirks, sort of an Edgar Allen Poe cat that had clambered up from the abyss of fright and raw pandemonium. I always suspected him of being the reincarnation of my old friend Ghengis Khan—something about the whiskers—but I couldn't get anybody else to agree, and he kept mum when I inquired. The big tom was as pitchy as the dark side of the moon, save for his splendid golden eyes. We ushered him into the hen yard with a high confidence in his abilities. At the first scent of rat pee, the fur along his spine went Mohawk and stood beautifully on end, and then he proceeded to levitate, arch, and spit clear across the chicken yard. And he crashed on those big gray rats like the unholy vengeance of Chaos and Old Night."

The little cat jumped down and showed him her tail as she eased out the screen door of the icehouse.

"I was just getting warmed up," he yelled. "I've got my own durn cow, you know—I could've been your ticket to milk twice a day." He hooted his derision, the sound rolling through the nearly empty icehouse. When the cat didn't return, he chugged down the rest of the beer.

"Damn untamable, unbribable felines."

Afterward, he walked home, whispering to himself and occasionally shadowboxing, wishing that the fellows had showed up. Once a girl shrieked, startled by his lungings and erratic footsteps.

"Oh!" The single cry shocked, the only unnatural note among the noises of a few crickets and the wind bowling dry leaves along the road.

"Hey! That's just Con Weaver." It was a boy's voice. He murmured something, and the girl burst into nervous laughter.

"Sorry, sorry. Didn't mean to scare you." Waving awkwardly, Conall hurried on into the small-town darkness. A flush of heat washed over him. He was so sure that the two were mocking him, talking about the crazy young writer who didn't have a normal job and rambled around town whenever he liked. Lived with his mama and daddy.... They didn't know that he had a letter in his pocket from Phillip Wildsmith, and probably they wouldn't recognize the name if they did.

"I don't care a damn what any of them think," he said, and began to shadowbox once more.

Yet the idea that he had frightened somebody—a girl, too!—disturbed him, and he soon stopped. He was quiet and restrained the rest of the way to the house, his arms swinging at his side. Although the dirty sluice of the boom had sent its guttersnipes sliding away toward the next oil strike, he still felt the town to be threatening, the night populated with bullies and roughnecks and whores and even lower life, scavengers and bottom-feeders trawling in the muck.

He could see the car parked in front, so Doc was back home after seeing a patient, maybe after having supper. The sound of the girl's voice echoed in memory, but he told himself that it was the coolness of the night that made him shiver. The shadowy womb of the house meant shelter, where he could curl up and be safe to drift in his own thoughts. Yet he felt a reluctance to go in, to lie down in the stifling air—as if he were going in to the family tomb!

Crossing the yard, he touched the letter in his pocket. Tonight, he promised himself, he would write to Wildsmith.

Inside the house, everything was terribly the same, here his mother declining in the sunken cushions, there his father whistling lightly in annoyance.

Pool of Time

The days and months streamed away, and everything seemed outwardly the same to Conall. It was a wonder how Cross Plains and his family could go on unchanged, and how he could change and change inwardly and no one ever notice. Boxing at the icehouse, he had won a place among the tougher elements of town, but there were few other haunts where he was hailed and respected for any reason. His mother and father encouraged him, yet he found that there was something missing in their attentions. At times, he felt irritated with their words of praise, or with Doc's pleasure in the money he was earning. Meanwhile, carbon copies of published and forthcoming stories mounted, along with letters from writers he had never met—the wooden cigar box had long ago overflowed with the latter.

It was a secret life he lived.

He was the invisible writer, the one who spun tales all the day long and was known in faraway places but never lauded at home. He was the prophet of doom and fair warning, scorned in his own country. He was the dadblame meritorious youth, never crowned with laurels, despised by the good people of the town.

The strange thing was this: nobody knew.

His own townspeople would have asked in astonishment and offense, "When did we fail to laud you? When did we ignore and scorn your prophecies? When did we forget to make a wreath of laurel and place it on your head?" They might have laughed, reeling back and forth, slapping their thighs at the idea that Doc's punkin-headed boy expected even the least acknowledgment of his poems and stories—as though those high-colored, feverish dreams could find a place among farmers and shopkeepers, oilmen and cowboys.

"Listen to this," one might have said, picking up a poem: "'Condemned like Lucifer to rage and fall, / These poems spark like shooting stars / That plumb the pitched infinities of all / That can appall the heart, or else enthrall / The soul with tales that close in grief and scars, / For war and Venus both belong to Mars.'"

"No dark infinities around these parts," another would reply. If they saw him, one might call out, "Hey, Sparky, set any stars on fire lately?"

Perhaps it was best that nobody knew...

Sometimes Conall thought that he lived from letter to letter, so keen a pleasure did he take in writing and receiving mail from his new friends, who understood regions of him that went unmapped in Texas. He dreamed of leaving home, dreamed of meeting these men on their home ground, dreamed of sailing across the sea to the Old World. These journeys appeared to him as wildest fantasy, each one ending with his mother abandoned in bed all day, white-faced and helpless, while his father joked with the townspeople and made rounds through the countryside.

Years back, Maeve had built her own little tower of isolation in Cross Plains. When new in town, she had insisted on those gold-rimmed plates for dinner parties. And when she spoke to the neighbors, she recalled (and sometimes mentioned) her myth of royal blood, letting a hint of Irish tinge her words. Consumptive and refined, she had erected a transparent but firm wall around herself, and few were allowed in.

"I owe her," Conall explained to his friends, "and she's better than this place."

Although he was aware of an anger that roiled in him when forced to admit the fetters that kept him at home, he did not examine the feeling closely. He was a Gulliver, lashed and tethered by a thousand Lilliputian demands. So it was, and so it remained, despite the occasional wrench and protest from the giant, who turned restlessly in sleep. A deep lethargy about all things other than his passions for writing and boxing kept him from tearing at the web that held him.

One night something woke him from a dream and, disoriented, he sat up in bed. The dim light showed him his books and papers, the unfolded sheets that were the latest letter from Wildsmith.

He swung his feet to the floor, glancing through what once was a window to the outside but was now the window that connected the porch bedroom to his mother's room. She was sleeping on her side in the faint glow from a bedside lamp. For a long time he sat, remembering the dream—dreams were useful to him.

"Old Yahweh," he said aloud.

He had been dreaming about a transparent blue pool, a crystalline figure seated on a stone at its center. Some bird had left droppings like silver tears on the man's shoulders. The droppings glittered in light that illuminated the pool, though all around lay darkness.

"Old Yahweh and the pool of time," he muttered, raking a hand through his hair.

Despite what seemed the best efforts of soapbox preachers to seed Conall's dreams with redemption and restoration, he had never once dreamed of Christ. Yahweh, however, paid him a night call from time to time.

And out in the darkness beyond the pool, the Norse gods roiled in the murk. Farther on, Ceres walked the world, her winter-white dress turning to a flush of spring's first gold as the chariot bearing her daughter jolted up the chasm that divided Hades from air and light. The districts of Conall's mind held other gods, less familiar, and powers of darkness never before named, who boiled up from the deep with mangled flesh in their jaws or lurked in labyrinths, the walls so deeply dyed by vermilion handprints that they seemed black.

When he woke in the night, he often felt his heart doing a quick footrace with panic until the world steadied and he knew exactly where he was.

But what had wakened him this time? He rubbed his face, remembering his long-ago alarm at an early-rising bird that had spent hours flying up and pecking the windowpanes on the side of the house.

"Fool bird."

A lady cardinal, the creature had wasted its energies fluttering against the glass, striking the panes with its persimmon-colored beak. As the dawn came up and sun flooded the walls, he sat watching the creature senselessly springing at the window, at each assault arching its wings and spreading its tail. For many weeks, she returned to batter the windows at odd hours of the day.

He got up and padded out of the room, roaming the house. The mean, bare furniture had gone silvery in the moonlight and reminded him of gilded tables and thrones in an Egyptian tomb. Even the couch had a sheen of silvery dust.

The noise that had must have roused him came again, and it was so familiar that he shook his head. It was his mother, coughing. She had wakened and gotten up in the dark. A dim triangle of light lay thrown onto the floor outside the bathroom.

Maeve's back was to him, the water running so that she didn't hear him. In the darkness with the one bulb burning, she looked unfamiliar, diminished and bent, lost inside the worn, faded-to-white gown. The walls, the sink, the figure, the reaching hand: all shone white on white on white. How snowy her hair had grown! That was the sickness, siphoning the color from her. A swirl of pity wrapped around him, and he regretted that he had been short with her earlier in the day.

The door to the medicine cabinet was ajar, and as she straightened, he glimpsed her face, its tired dark eyes and the mouth bloody, the cheek smeared. Although he might have expected such a picture, he started and almost cried out. He shrank from the image, first covering his eyes with his forearm but just as quickly jerking the arm down and taking a step away from the threshold. A dread kindred to that he had met in his stories when wandering underground in uncanny places made him tremble with cold. The sounds of the water gyring in the sink and gurgling through the pipes followed him, magnified unnaturally, and he broke into a sweat as he turned away, fleeing for refuge.

In the porch room, he lay down on his bed with one hand pressed close over the thud of his heart. Caradog shoved his wet nose into the other hand, worming closer and making a faint, querulous noise in his half-sleep. No, that was not real and could never be real because the dog was dead. Deprivation smote him. The world was loss, forever and ever, a long falling-away from the moments of infancy and ignorance when he had been held safe against a beating heart.

Conall would not tell himself what he had thought when he saw his mother's face. He would not go to that dark place with its winding corridors of blood and its nightmare fears. Instead, he emptied himself of everything, blanking out each image until all the world and its grids of civilization shone as a peaceful white, and every mazy confusion in his mind was obliterated.

Then he slept, perhaps to dream.

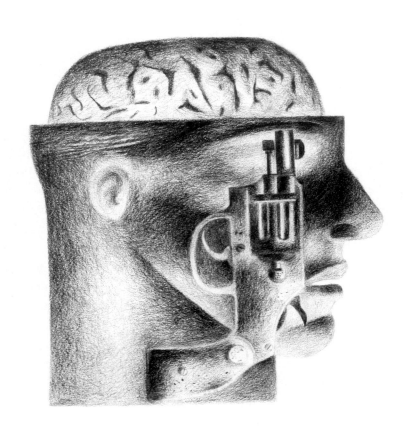

Child in the Bloodroot Maze

An Explosion in Heaven

A detonation far up in the piled thunderheads slammed him awake. A stench like the last century's *lucifer matches* swept through the room. The hair on the crown of his head stirred as barbed lightning sprang past the window and torched an oak tree. Little Conall was staying with his aunt and her half-Indian husband near Crystal City, there wasn't a screen in the house, and the first event that he could never forget was just about to happen. He was four, old enough to stand up on the sway-backed bed but young enough to tumble out the window as he leaned forward.

He flopped on his back in the weeds just as brightness ran like a tear down the face of night, trailing blue fireworks that made him freeze and stare in the dry, rattling grass. Half-naked people pounded across the yard, shouting against unseen enemies. Someone fired a gun. The unknown gleam exploded with flame once again before colliding with earth, its impact shaking the ground. Conall's fingers closed over a piece of quartz jutting from the soil and gripped until his palm bloomed stigmata.

The burst of fire had sounded to him like an enormous ragged cough. It frightened him and made him think of blood. Largeness and loneliness of the night entered in, hollowing out the child until nothing was left but a bare vessel, whistling in the winds from the cosmos. He could not even muster a cry that might bring his mother with her smell of rose water and her encircling arms. Rigid, the child lay like a toppled statue, wrapped in a caul of mosquito netting.

A mockingbird woke and let out a series of rasps and trills from its perch in a soapberry tree. He heard somebody shout. Then he saw the uncle's blue-lit face close to his, and he was thrust bodily back through the window.

Breath returned, puffing in and out of his small lungs. Slowly his heart ceased to shudder. He remembered the blue fires in the sky without dying. But the world had changed for him in one star-struck moment. Its mystery had crashed in on him, torn a trench through the safe precincts of home. Conall groped through his small store of knowledge, searching for news about what had happened to the sky and earth. It would be a long time before he rummaged up the right answer. Now he stared out the window at the rich cloak of night, scattered with stars.

The boy had heard stories enough from his grandmothers that he pictured the Lord God in a robe and with a sparkly white beard, hurling Satan down to hell. But could *Texas* be hell? Already he sensed that the word meant more than could be fathomed.

Seed of Aunt Lachesis

"Tell about when Old Missus passed."

"Old Missus? Why you want to hear about that bad woman again? Why you like Aunt Lachesis stories? You trying to figure something out? You been meeting up with bad women? They's all kind of bad women in the world. Catch you in their claws. Missus was one. White people thought she was married to the master. Huh. She married the devil. Long, long back she was a fine young girl. Pretty. Uh-huh. You know what that word *daguerrotype* means? There was one of them things in the parlor, and once I picked it up and got a good look. Showed Old Missus about seventeen years old in her wedding suit, with a tee-tiny waist—looked like what they called a wasp waist, like she couldn't get no breath. Maybe didn't need none. Had a sting."

Conall hugged his knees to his chest. Stories told by Aunt Lachesis Jones always crawled under his skin and sunk their hooks into his flesh. Once Doc Weaver had treated an adventurer who had spent a year in Central America, and whose body knew the bad luck of being chosen as the egg lair for a devilish jungle parasite. Doc had told the man to keep his skin coated with a thick layer of petroleum jelly, so thick that the emerging creatures would be forced to keep boring toward the air. It took months for the infant monsters to chew bolt holes out of his knee. After that he jagged along with a limp, and the oil companies wouldn't hire him for drilling work. That's what Auntie's stories were like—what the horror of them felt like—and they were almost as terrible as the tales from his two grandmothers that shadowed his playtime and dreams. Once when he launched a pebble at a red-winged blackbird with a slingshot, his mother's mother told him how her husband the Colonel had survived the war between the states, only to kill the whippoorwills that were like to drive him mad with their mournful calls. He made it through all that bloodshed, and then to be cursed by one family death after another.... Never harm a whippoorwill! The other grandmother muttered tales about a horseless wagon heaped with arms and legs, a dream horse that climbed the stairs to where someone lay dying inside a plantation house with the roof caving inward and the ghosts of mourning doves cooing in the ivy on the chimney. In his dreams, the death horse was saddled to the wagon, and the doves grieved as heads and arms were tossed from the upper windows of the mansion.

"Tell about Old Missus's face."

"In the daguerrotype, she had this stiff little smile, but her eyes was deer eyes—big and kind of frightened. She didn't seem so bad. Like she could've been gentle. But she didn't stay gentle-looking. So that picture gave me the heebie-jeebies. You ever seen a doll with a painted mouth and big glass eyes that made your skin creep? After he got tired of that wasp waist, Old Master got to slipping off to the cabins—"

"Why did he do that?"

Aunt Lachesis Jones and Conall were sitting on the barely-warm stove, their feet tucked up. She looked him up and down. It was the first time he had thought to ask about the master's prowlings.

"You'll find out sooner or later. Sooner if you stick with me. Why not now?" She paused, considering, and then gave a jerk of the head, as if agreeing. "You seen dogs on dogs? Or a bull humping on a cow?

Maze of Blood

He was going down there for the girls. Go lie on top of naked gals and shove his hambone inside."

"Did you ever see it?"

"His hambone? Sure I did. He'd whap it out any time he wanted. Don't you be thinking about doing that stuff, you hear? It's my sure-set convicted word that bad men get their peckers shrunk up. That thing'll fix to dissolve if you get it damped down too often."

The boy pondered this piece of news. Evidently here was another reason not to bathe.

"Old Missus was the very most jealousest woman that I ever saw. She married the master, and after that she sure enough made her a bigamy and married the devil. You know bigamy? That's doing big game, when you marry more than one. Jacob's Annie said she saw Satan himself give the missus a ring, the two of them standing right in front of the parlor fireplace on the hearth rug. He was eight feet tall with brass horns, and his skin clanged like a bell when Old Missus put her hand on his thigh."

"Did you see him?"

"Me? Huh. I don't want nothing to do with no bad angels. I had enough to do with them temptations Satan kept whispering into Old Master's ear. Tickling his hairy ear morn and night."

"What did he say?"

"The devil was always budging in, telling the master to slide on down to the cabins and make some frolic."

"What frolic?"

"Did you hear me say? Gone to the cabins to chase girls. Wasn't much of a chase. It was flop down and spraddle or else get whipped, and either way the master had him a high old time. He used to order me to go and fetch him some of that special sweet water from the spring, and then he'd cut around and stop me in the mesquite patch. Always had him a rolled-up blanket on his saddle. Uh-huh. You don't want too many women, boy. You know what I'm saying? That's sin. Mortal sin. More-tail sin, my Uncle Cephus used to say."

"Why?"

"Just look at the master. Chasing. Catching. Always wanting more, more. That man's mouth was always watering. Kiss it, you'd go to tasting metal. Devil brass. My cousin told my grandbaby Ruby that the devil gave Old Master a charm bracelet—you know what a charm bracelet is?—and on every link dangled a silver gal. You know what silver does? Tarnish? Tarnish makes it go black. Black gals is what he had. 'Course that was just a way of talking. He didn't have nothing on his wrist but hair and more hair. You can't see the kind of bracelet the devil puts on a man. *Manacles* is what them kind is called. So don't you go taking too many women when your britches get big. It'll sure enough suck out your soul, Conny."

Conall nodded when she peered into his face. He wasn't really listening. He was more interested in Old Missus than the Master because Aunt Lachesis Jones had called her a witch.

"You never told how she died."

He waited for an answer, slowly inspecting her face, leaning close to breathe in her fragrance of burnt sugar and molasses. People said that Auntie Lachesis had been beautiful once. She was whiter than his own mother, but somewhere in her swam a minnow-drop of African blood that had condemned her to labor and to lie spread eagle in a grove of mesquite trees for a bad master.

"Missus? Hoo! I didn't think she could die, her being a witch and all." The old woman shook out her dress and let her skinny legs dangle off the edge of the stove. She reached for her tin of dip and packed a pinch of snuff between her lip and gum.

"So how did she?" Conall tugged at her skirts.

"One day Old Missus took sick, and she told a couple of slave gals to stand around her bed with turkey feather fans and keep the air moving. Shoot-fire, it was hot and still! Me and Bessie was carrying water out to the hands in the cotton field. Not our job but we toted water all the same. It looked like the end of the world—the heat waving on the horizon so's you 'spected somebody bad was coming toward you at a run.

"Master was out on the porch, leaning over the rail, and he didn't let out a peep when we went by, even though I had on a cast-off dress he give me and looked a sight better in it than Old Missus ever did. Didn't even slap me or Bessie on the rump. Maybe he was pondering on all those nights he'd been messing in the cabins, making his bride fry with hate until she leaned over the hearth and yelled into the sparks and the devil flew down the chimney like a firebird. I didn't say a word to Old Master, neither. If I'd had my druthers, I'd just a-kept on with walking till I found out the sea. I'd sure like to wade in the waves. But I didn't get no druthers. I had a jar on my head, and water trickled onto my face and neck and shot down my dress and gave me some cool. Maybe I let it slosh out that way on purpose."

Aunt Lachesis picked up a coffee can and spat.

"The hoed-up dirt dusted fire-sparks on my bare soles. Missus came into my mind, how she'd done been parched by anger till she got to looking as grooved and gray as the busted-up table under the pecan trees where Bessie and me set down the jars. I felt a mite sorry for her, just for a minute. If only the master had been good to her! But he wasn't ever good to nobody—and I mean *nobody*! Liquid slopped out, and them old dry boards drank it. Overseer told the hands in the high cotton to go on, and they started drifting along my way. Then something strange happened. Heads all over the field bobbled up as a blast came a-rumpling and a-rampling across the world. Hit me just like a slap and made me shiver with the furnace heat. The gals in the rows set up a whoop of *glory hallelujah!* because they knowed Old Man Satan had come to fetch the missus and was riding her carriage bones down to hell."

The boy twitched, and a driblet of perspiration slipped erratically through his hair like a metal bead rolling and catching in a child's maze puzzle.

"Conall?"

Maeve leaned in the kitchen doorway, a handkerchief balled in her fist. A straw hat threw a shadow over her face, and against the glare of the open door her body looked black and solid.

The boy let out a squeak of alarm. He didn't want to leave, but his mama didn't like him to spend too much time in the kitchen. Colored people and white people weren't the same, she had told him. Each had their ways of doing, and the ways of one were not the ways of the other.

"Conall, what are you bothering Aunt Lachesis for?"

"Conny ain't no bother, Miz Maeve," the old woman said comfortably, dredging the tin of snuff from her pocket.

"I ain't no bother. See?"

"Now, Conall, don't you sass me," Maeve cautioned, holding out her hand. "You come on along."

The boy stared at her, his eyes unblinking and mouth ajar. When he didn't move, she began to clear her throat and then to cough, seizing the frame of the door as if she needed support. He quivered, hearing a liquid sound inside her neck, and the familiar panic unfurled in his chest. It was a blood-dipped flag of terror that signaled death and destruction to his mother—her corpse like a wickless candle in a pine box and the world gone barren. Often he had run to her, fearing her dress would be soaked with blood, or else had leaned close while she slept, listening for the draw of her breath. He had a queer superstitious sense that his presence kept her alive, that the two of them were joined by awful links that could not be shattered without destroying both of them. At first a nervous tension, half a childish passion for her embrace and half fright, held him from going to her. But as the spasms of coughing grew stronger, he broke from Aunt Lachesis and flung himself onto Maeve, seizing her around the waist and shoving his face against the bodice of her gown. After a little while the coughs quieted, and she straightened up and led him away.

When he looked back over his shoulder, Aunt Lachesis was staring after them, her mouth crooked up at one corner. Maybe that was the snuff. She saw him looking at her and winked.

In the parlor, mother and son played a game of Chinese checkers. Maeve's milky blue marbles trounced his red ones. She laughed and offered to play again.

"How'd you do that?" Conall clicked a few of the red marbles in his hand.

"Maybe it was magic." She gave him a sidelong look. "Maybe I'm a sorceress like the ones in that old woman's stories."

She was teasing him, he was almost sure.

"You're not coughing anymore," he said.

"No."

For the first time, a cloud of doubt came into his thoughts. Perhaps his mother had been fooling him. It might be that she was good at forcing somebody to her will, the way Old Missus and Old Master had been. Perhaps she just had a different manner, quiet but persistent.

"Mama," he said, "do you know what a charm bracelet is?"

Buckskin Callahan Has His Say

People ought not bust out and go gallivantin' around like roosters. Why, that Doc Weaver couldn't have rested his haunches in one place for more'n a year in a row until that boy of his was in double digits. Allus thought he'd get rich, trailin' after one cussed boom town after another, totin' that woman Maeve after him, and maybe her as bad as him about havin' itchy feet that couldn't be still. Start tappin', and before you know it, them Weavers done fired off over the county line and sot down somewheres else. Cotton boom, cattle boom, oil boom, boom boom boom!

KAPOW!

That kinda thing is bewilderfyin' to young'uns.

This poor babe popped onto the scene in Peaster, but afore he knowed his name, he was a bone-i-fied resident of Seminole, over New Mexico way. Purty soon, they all three had the tongues hangin' out their heads like bell clappers. Wasn't no water to be had, so they hopped to Bagwell, over in the piney woods, 'cause they's plenty of liquid refreshment along that way. They found water, all right, but so dern much that the ground took on a skin of green, and the rain didn't let up for three months, and one day the fishes was swimmin' in the washout by the road, and the next week the fishes was in the durn road. Soon the fishes went to swimmin' in the piney woods, flippin' with big ole belly flops from tree to tree like they felt called upon to be circus acrobats.

That boy and Aunt Lachesis Jones would haul up on the cold stove and sit with their feet drugged up, and she would set his hair on fire with stories about slave-time, and how Old Witch Missus carried a lash and was out of her cotton-pickin' mind jealous of the slave gals. Aunt Lachesis was high, high yaller—she was just nothing but one-sixteenth color or less, maybe, but that didn't make no nevermind. She still was no more'n a slave back in the bad old days.

Miz Arabella, she'd wade over to the kitchen with a little pigtailheaded pickaninny holding an umbreller over her head like she was a queen of lions and rhino cirruses back in Africa. She was the founder, owner, and no. 1 operator of *The Sanctification & Sanitation Laundry*. She'd collect the clothes to be scrubbed on the washboard, and then she'd get to jawkin' with Conall and Aunt Lachesis, all of 'em perched up there on the stove while the little gal with the umbreller waded ankle-deep. Miz Arabella done witnessed to both of them as they were sittin' on the stove about how she crossed over to the Lord God in slave-time over black mountains and red mountains and how she was hanged for three fire-breathing days in the cobwebs on the sure-fire Gates of Hell until the sweet Lord Jesus brought her a drop of dew to drink. Her lips that were all parched and cracked went to kissing that precious tear. What was that stuff to put in a little feller's mind? Them tales of Aunt Lachesis was all over him when it came time for dreamin', and that boy would walk, talk, and holler s'bad at night that the Weavers' place was as rackety as a bunkhouse birthday. Even though Doc Weaver drug Maeve and the boy off somewheres else soon enough, the Lachesis Jones stories stuck burr-tight.

It got so if it was Mond'y, it was Dark Valley Creek; if it was Tuesd'y, must be the Palo Pinto Hills; if it was Wednesd'y, it must be Atascosa County; and on Sund'y they'd probably stray nigh Oklahoma or Missouri. Oh, he had the adventures, all right. Got fired up by fire ants. Rattled by rattlers. Blistered on the alkali plains. Got locked accidental-like in a stinkin' backhouse until he couldn't yell no more and afterward had the fantods at night, dreaming about that dark devil throat choked with corruption. All the time Doc Weaver was out chewin' the fat with his patients, tellin' wild tales, and sittin' down to home-cooked meals at strangers' tables. His wife Maeve hunkered at home, coughin' up a mite or more of blood and playin' the tragedy queen.

Soon she got to dreamin' that she was from a sure-enough line of queens, and that made her better than the doctor and the people roundabout and everybody except her son, because he was descended from royalty, too. The pair of them had glory and martyrdom piled on their heads like never-endin' crowns. Nobody in all of Texas could live up to such secret, exultacious, and grandifying Gaelic glory. Irishness was starting to be downright pop'lar—the queer thing being that not fifty years back, the Irish was scorned and heaped together with the Africans as the most lowdown and misbegotten unfortunates in the country.

That hapless sprat just had to hang on for the roisterin' Weaver ride. Life was all perambulatin' the wilderness with his mama and daddy. Once he was torn away by a yellow-green dirt devil while Maeve ran scritchin' after him until the little twister dumped him in a heap of buffalo chips. If you don't believe in devils, Texas weather'll change your mind—surgin' around and knockin' down walls.

Poor old Con had about the queerest dern upbringing you could feature. One night him and his folks were off visiting, and that little fella was sleepin' the sweet sleep of the just and young in a house that belonged to his Aunt Reenie and her half-Injun husband, Farrell, when *KABOOM!* the boy sat up in bed squawkin' for his mama. The world had gone blue and done been blowed to pieces. The menfolks jumped for guns, thinkin' that some of Farrell's business associates had gone and chunked sticks of dynamite under the house—it was just a shack hoisted up on brick posts to keep off the termites. Came to find out it wasn't the end of time but a meteorite as big as a baby hippopotamus.

I cain't rightly say how big a hippopotamus infant is, but I'd guess a right smart of a size.

Maeve kept that boy locked up at home, the two hardly even goin' out to Sunday School. Wouldn't let him play, unless it was with a boy from a high-falutin' family. Sometimes he went on rounds with his pa, and then his ma would drag herself out of the house and ride with them, though she was worn to a sliver by time she got home. He was trapped in there with that female lovin' him ever dadblame minute of the day until it was plumb tiresome, and her coughin' up TB blood s'nasty-like, makin' him go wild with the heebie-jeebies for fear she'd up and die and leave him locked in the house with nothing but a pop-eyed, bloody-mouthed corpse and miles and miles of bare-bones Texas for company. That'd be one awful bughouse addlement.

And when that boy did swing out the door, it generally meant time for a move. Them three wasn't nothin' but tumbleweeds rollin' to the next post, twiddlin' on a strand of barbed wire. Enough to get my dander roused, just thinkin' about that misfortunate squirt of a boy.

Doomed to dream up friends like ol' Buckskin Callahan.

Doomed to turn out squirrelly.

Ain't that right?

The Sunday School Boy

When his mother fell asleep, Conall tiptoed around the rocker, sliding the two-legged pins out of her hair until it loosened and began to spill over her shoulders. If she had gone back to bed, he would have crawled in and nestled against her until the warmth settled him into sleep, but she had dropped into a doze as she read aloud from *Kidnapped*. He liked it when they drifted into slumber while reading on the coverlet, but he didn't like this: her head was cocked back, mouth yawning open onto darkness and an odor of old blood. Looking inside, he had seen the dark place where a tooth was missing and now didn't glance again. He was comfortable with her hair and body, but he didn't want to see her face, looking like a stranger's. The blackness in her mouth made him uneasy. If he could go as small as a pin and climb on two crooked legs down the throat, he would hobble through the corridors of her body and find the death that had seeded itself in her lungs and was turning them to an evil lace.

He lay on the floor and walked the hairpins along the cracks in the boards until he lost interest. Having sprinkled them at her feet, he got up, hunting for something to do. Restless, he pawed through a few books, stopping to examine an occasional picture, and then wandered into her room. In the flowered dish on her dresser, he found more of the crooked pins, along with a string of coral beads, a marcasite shirt pin, and the nubs of yellowing baby teeth—macabre, stained with time and looking as if they had come out of a grave instead of his own mouth.

He felt as if something were tiptoeing across him—some little shield bug, maybe, tickling his skin with its feet—yet it wasn't that exactly. He looked around the room, glimpsing himself drowned and wavery in the mirror's depths. What was it? He thought about getting out a pot lid and poker to defend the house, but it was so hot that he didn't feel like going outside to the summer kitchen. Somebody would be watching. He was the new kid in town again, a thing that always made him feel blue. Pushing a curtain aside, he peeped into the yard.

A boy was standing in front of the steps, his head cocked, staring straight up as if he'd known Conall would be coming to the window.

He had red hair that had been slept on vigorously and stuck outward in contrary directions. His snub nose and pot-handle ears seemed to augur cheerfulness.

Conall recognized him as the kid from Sunday School who had been sent to a chair in the corner for too much whispering when the teacher was reading a story about a man who was swallowed by a whale. He'd been barefoot and wearing overalls with no shirt, and that was how he was still dressed.

Going out on the porch, Conall carefully pulled the door shut and stared some more, not speaking.

"What's your name?"

"Conall." The word tumbled out of his mouth like an oversized aggie. He didn't think to ask for a name in return.

"Mine's Herbert. Want to play?" The boy grinned at him.

He nodded.

"Cowboys and Indians?"

"All right," Conall said, glancing over his shoulder. Maeve would be asleep for a few hours, and Doc had been called away in the night and might not be back for a long while. "See those trees? Let's go down there."

Herbert moved quick and low, darting toward him so fast that Conall panicked and dashed away. For some time they ran back and forth, tagging each other with stick hatchets. Using an ancient penknife fished from Herbert's bib pocket, they peeled branches for guns and spears and spent some time squatting in the shade, searching for pointed pebbles to tie onto their weapons with grasses and thread yanked from the hem of the overalls.

"Let's be Comanches," Conall suggested.

"Sure."

"I'd like to be a Comanche when I grow up," he added, admiring a gray stone lashed to a peeled stick.

"I'm going to be a cowboy," Herbert said stoutly.

Their bloodthirsty yells were swallowed by the huge Texas sky. They dashed around the trees, flinging spears and lurching to the ground whenever nicked by a stone. It was the most fun Conall had had in a long time. Not until he saw his father swinging down from a farmer's mule-drawn wagon did they stop. The boys hid the gear under the house and arranged for Herbert to come back the following afternoon.

The rest of the day he daydreamed about their hours together, and on the next morning woke eager for more.

When he glimpsed the boy waiting in front of the house, he hurried to the door, but his mother had beaten him onto the porch. She had a fountain pen in one hand. That meant she had been writing a letter.

"My son is not available," she was saying to Herbert.

"Yes, I am!" He flung himself out the door, grinning at his new friend.

"Oh, there you are," she said, frowning.

Maeve went to the edge of the porch, hand on hips, and examined Herbert. He smiled uneasily, his hand going to the bib pocket where

Conall had seen a stash of rabbit tobacco and a package of papers.

"How do you know Conall?"

"Sunday School," he said, looking surprised. He dug in the dirt with his bare toes, ducking his head.

"Well, Conall is busy this afternoon."

"No, I'm not, Mama."

"No, ma'am," she corrected. "And yes, you are. I need my son's help. Where do you come from, child?"

Conall tugged at her apron. "I want to play."

Herbert bobbed his head again. "Mommer and Daddy work the old Pruett farm. It's about a mile down the road."

"Sharecroppers, you mean?"

"Yes'm," he whispered.

She shook her head. "He can't be playing today or tomorrow. He's got more important work to do."

"No, no, I don't." Conall was dancing up and down, anxious to race in the heat and to lie in the shade to rest, playing with sticks and pebbles.

"Don't deny me," she said in a low voice.

He looked at the patch of trees. The play place seemed farther away than it had the day before.

"Mama, we had us a good time with cowboys and Indians." He yanked on her arm, desperate to make her understand.

She clicked her tongue.

"Indians! Enough. You run along, Herbert. Maybe you two will see each other when you're nine and start school."

"We'll probably move, and I'll never see him again," Conall said.

"Nonsense." She waved briskly at the boy, who had already turned away and was scuffing the dirt with his bare foot. "I'll read you a story when I get to a stopping place."

"We always move." Conall, too, kicked at the ground, sending up a puff of dust.

"I wonder if that child has lice. They've cropped his hair off mighty short. These sharecropper children always have something you don't want to catch—ringworm or pinkeye or something," Mama declared.

"No! He didn't have anything like that! We had fun. What's so wrong about having some fun? We made things and played games. We had us a swell time."

"We have each other, son. What do we need for strangers? Low, no-count people."

It was no use.

Conall flung himself through the open door and ran toward his room. Parting the curtains, he saw that Herbert was shuffling along, head bowed. The glare of the sun whitened the ground where he walked and made the stubble on his head into a stiff halo. He looked smaller now, the shoulders narrow in the too-big overalls. Once he stopped and looked back. A little later, he squatted to watch something happening on the ground.

Conall wanted to see. Maybe an ant war. Maybe they were dragging a dead baby rattlesnake or a puffy, gold-horned grub. Maybe a monster cicada.

When the boy's shape dwindled and was lost from sight, Conall hurled himself onto the bed, eyes stinging.

"I hate you," he whispered to the pillow. "I hate you, and I'll never, ever love you." Even as the words fell from his mouth, Conall knew that they weren't true, that everything was more complicated than he could explain.

For a long time he lay with his head buried under the sack of feathers. Even so, he could hear his mother moving around in the next room. After a while, she began to cough.

Like a Meteorite

The boy was twelve, reveling in the strange dust-smelling murk of a New Orleans library, watching motes flash gold in a beam of sun. He loved the ceiling lights on chains and the table lamps with their green glass shades. The room was as beautiful as another world. The silky wood of the worn library table felt cool on his arms. To him, the library tables looked as though a magic-worker had cut a pool of murky water into slabs, the corners rounded because the caramel-colored liquid refused to be sharp. The mage had let the liquid settle into tabletops, and the words of the spell seethed in the curves of grain that had once been ripples. The surface appeared as still and effortless as a windless pool, but it was only illusion because the words of the spell had to harangue and corral the molecules of water to keep the tables in place.

"That's it," Conall whispered. Every inch of this magical chamber was governed by words.

Perhaps all of the world's life had been spoken into being—who could say?

He thumbed the gilt letters on a spine, *The Romance of Early British Life*, letting their richness and the words send a message through his fingers before he opened the book.

After a while he closed his eyes and lost himself in daydream. The millions of leaves bound between covers unloosed themselves and floated into a canopy above the carved pillars. His feet pattered on the understory. He began to lope for the pure joy of it, though he sensed that there was, nevertheless, some reason to be moving forward. Stray pages swirled to the floor, piling and decaying, returning to a primordial alphabet soup. When he glimpsed a boy his own age, he hurried faster. Shadows stirred among the litter, deepened and darkened the corridor through the forest. Overhead, the black letters on leaves faded, turned to holes eaten by insects, and let light in through branches. The road curled on between stacks of highland stone and towering virgins, decked in gold needles or green-glass leaves.

Out there—he could sense them, hiding behind the trees—moved a jumble of Celtic tribes, and the descendants of even earlier peoples, all enemies of the slight, dark-skinned figure and his kind. A feathery rush of feeling for these ancient barbarian peoples swept through him, making him quiver with unexpected joy.

Sweat stung his eyes as he caught sight of the boy's face turned to his and the sharpened stick in one hand. For an instant the features blurred with the long-ago image of his uncle in the night, gleaming blue under the strange light of an exploding star.

The blue tattoos smoldered in the shade of the stacks, wrapping like letters around the cheekbone, along the jaw.

Picts. *Picti*, the painted people.

But it wasn't his uncle's strangely lit image in the young Pict's face... With a shiver, he understood. This story, like that one, belonged to him. The face was his own, made strange, as if in a mirror of bronze.

The blue-tattooed boy leaped around the feet of standing stones. Close by, a woman pressed her body against the cold corrugated rock, whispering a love song to the earth, murmuring to barbarian gods who had never yet heard rumors of their twilight and death.

"Stonehenge," the library dreamer whispered.

A wizard lifted his arms to the sun as it bounced above the line of the horizon like a bobber of fire jerked and then let go by a cosmic fish. The Pictish boy crouched, his blue markings standing out like fresh scars, and shrank away. He looked about furtively, once again catching the dreamer's eye. They stared and seemed to recognize that each would have something to do with the other, somewhere in the future, as if—

A hand clasped his shoulder.

"Conall, you ready to go? Look at all these books you dragged out."

He let out a sharp cry of surprise that made the librarians look his way, and the pretty one with the sheaf of blonde hair shushed him with a smile.

"Come on, now—the lectures are done for the morning, and we need to get us some dinner." The doctor clapped his son on the back. The two of them had talked and told stories and laughed for most of the long trip, yet now the father appeared like an intruder in the library.

For Conall, the trip had been magicked away by books and dreams more intense than the memory of Doc beaming at him as they labored in the hot sun at the side of the road. The boy's momentary pride in helping change the tire, the picnic under a live oak with fried chicken and hard-boiled eggs and fruitcake with pecans, the hoots of laughter as they barely missed a scuttling armadillo: these memories had fallen like dead astral leaves into a crater on the dark side of the moon.

Even the direct appeal of father to son, made somewhere between home and New Orleans, had been lost. "We might ought to spend more time together, just us two fellows," Doc Weaver had said, nodding toward the yellow and green sunbursts of insects on the windshield.

"Sure," Conall said. He felt the tug of loyalty to his mother, but it snapped and sailed away like spider's silk.

A beetle hit the glass with a loud spang! that made them jump.

"Big'un," Doc said. "Thought it was a gunshot, there for a second."

"That'd be bad." The boy craned out the window to check for bank robbers on the lam. The straight Texas road stretched out behind them like the definition of forever.

"We don't want guns going off in the car, do we, son?"

"No, sir." He didn't listen to what his father had to tell him about there being a time and a place for everything but raked the bangs back from his eyes. His scalp felt sore where the wind had twisted his hair.

Bangs, he thought. *Odd how the same syllable can mean clipped hair and the bark of a gun.*

"What I was asseverating, when I was so unceremoniously ejected from my smoothly-running train of thought by that rambunctious flying missile of a dadgum green-blooded bug—"

The car drifted back and forth across the empty highway as Doc strung together his lively, ornate words. They caught Conall's interest.

"Yes, sir?"

"—was that a man and his son ought not to be tied up too tight by apron strings, if you take my meaning. Stallion and colt need to kick up their heels without a mare along to blight all the fun."

"A mare—"

"Not that your mother doesn't mean to do good," Doc added hastily, "because she does. But maybe there's a little too much fancified-doing-the-fine-thing, since too much fuss and fustian can make folks uncomfortable."

"Why—"

"No, no, I don't speak one blessed word against your mama. Maeve's a sure enough crackerjack as a mother. It's just that maybe she's a little too—even crackerjacks get stale after a while, don't they?

And then you maybe feel like having a red-hot chili pepper and some onion along with your lady peas. Or maybe a nice bit of barbeque brisket. You get my meaning, son?"

He cast the boy a glance and leaned forward, letting his damp shirt pull away from the seat.

"I guess so," Conall said. He reached up and rubbed at the fine necklace made of dust and sweat at his throat. The beads rolled away under his thumb.

"Aw, forget I said anything," Doc had exclaimed.

And so the boy did, along with most of the long, hot journey that his father had promised would be so important to them both.

Now he stared at the man as though at a stranger.

Conall stood up, trembling a little, and looked about the long room with its green glass shades and golden hanging lamps. The dream hung on, lending the long aisles between the stacks an alluring shadowiness. He hardly remembered why they had come to Louisiana or that his father would be taking him back home when the medical seminars were ended.

The infinite library wandered on forever, calling his name.

The Swing and the Maze

But oh! That deep romantic chasm which slanted
Down the green hill athwart a cedarn cover!
A savage place! as holy and enchanted
As e'er beneath a waning moon was haunted
By woman wailing for her demon-lover!

Maeve was whispering the poem to her son while he worked the porch swing monotonously back and forth, thrusting now from the porch rail, now from the painted floor. The act had a hypnotic fascination for him, made him feel calm and settled. Many times Conall had heard his mother recounting how the ancestral voices prophesying war had come to Kubla Khan from afar, so he drifted in and out of consciousness of the words and of her hand rubbing his back. The cotton shirt clung to the skin between his shoulders. He smelled female sweat and gardenia powder and the faint odor of decay from his mother's illness. Blood streaked the balled-up handkerchief in her lap.

Heavily bored, he kicked off hard and shut his eyes, remembering the dazzling white cemeteries of Louisiana and tombs like marvelous playhouses for children, set on narrow streets paved with oyster shells, bleached and burning in the sun....

In memory, the narrow streets of the dead felt hotter than Texas.

Mugginess lifted from the ground, dampening his clothes, making him feel greasy with sweat. He picked up a fallen branch and began to pound along the oyster shell paths, his feet crushing the shards underfoot as his father shouted for him not to get lost. But he became disoriented in the maze of the dead. The stick sparkled with salt crystals and was sometimes a sword and sometimes a wand in his hand. Drenched with moisture that seemed to accompany him like a moving cloud, he ran until he could not hear the voice calling his name.

Stopping, he glanced around at the bone-white brilliance of marble and plastered river brick. A tiny plaque with an angel or fairy standing tiptoe in the trumpet of a flower drew his eye. Beside the threshold of a tomb, a veiled figure bent low in mourning. Nearby, a mockingbird broke into trills, twisting a ribbon of notes until it curled with joy. Seized by a thought, Con pressed his ear against the wall of a mausoleum, but all he could hear was the blood surging in his veins. Then he knelt and listened at a carved wooden chest left as an offering next to a vase of sun-bleached cloth flowers and a tin pennywhistle. After a moment, he distinguished the fine, small chewing of termites that had awakened him the night before in his rented room. The wooden lid was spongy under his hand, and when he drew his fingers back, a sliver fell away, and pale golden shapes nosed at the air.

He trudged on, shivering a little with heat and disgust, striking his weapon at the doors of the buildings and mentally commanding the occupants to come forth. Nobody did, though he imagined that they might be shifting in their pale shrouds. He thought about Lazarus, already stinking, called back from the land of the dead. Jesus had hated death. He had jerked the dead back to life.

The stick rattled along ironwork bars. He could hear his father again, the voice coming to him as if from underwater.

Surely he was near the secret heart of the maze! He thought of the irregular grid of shell walkways, the white city of the dead inside a living city moated by swamp and sea and river. How different it was from anything in the crooked, four-pointed star that was his home state. Perhaps Texas, too, was a labyrinthine region, though its paths were mostly invisible.

"A red maze."

Red for the blood of frontiersmen and Indians, he thought, *red for the blood of heroes and mother, the martyr of Cross Plains. Maze for the looping coils of a snake that ended in a rattle that shook warning: don't tread on me! Maze for veins of blood. Maze for family.* Obscene and unbidden, the question came to him in a rush. *Why do I love her more than him, despite how she is?*

Another question tried to take shape, something about what to be and how to choose. In it, the manliness of Doc Weaver was all mixed up with the soft fabric of fantasy that wrapped his wife. But the question had no more clarity than a knot sketched in loose sand.

"Maze." His thoughts flicked once more to Texas.

A denuded landscape like a desert or an over-grazed prairie was a kind of maze, though it had no door. A man or a boy could go missing there and find the nothingness at its heart and be eaten alive.

He wouldn't tell his father. Doc didn't like such thoughts. "You spend too much time with your mother," he often said. But it was hard not to imagine strange things when Maeve's body was a kind of living tomb and her lungs were as tattered as his great-grandmother's reticules, chewed by insects. They made another kind of maze, one where even the air could get lost.

He stood quietly, listening to the birds and a mysterious tapping sound, his face relaxed and still. Yet a fanciful passerby might have been arrested by the look of the boy, finding the mouth wounded and oversensitive and something sorrowful in the deep-set eyes.

The city of the dead is listening to me, and I am listening to it.

And what is in the heart of the maze?

Maze of Blood

The repetitive noise now compelled his whole attention. With a thrill of surprise, he saw someone step into the narrow alleyway between the tombs. He, too, had a stick, a long one like a wizard's staff. With it he was tapping, tapping at the oyster shell, at times brushing against a mausoleum, feeling it with his hands.

Conall watched him come forward. The figure was enormous, heavily muscled and big-shouldered, cradling a sheaf of sturdy daisies and zinnias in his arms. He wore a black suit, wrong for the weather, right for his errand. Perspiration had sprung out on a face the color of burned caramel, and tinted glasses had slipped down on his nose to reveal bald white orbs. A rivulet of sweat flowed from one staring eye to the jaw, as if he had been weeping, though the boy felt sure he never shed tears.

"Who's there?" The man didn't pause—just simply mowed down the air with a swing of his arm.

Toppling onto the shells, Conall cried out once and lay still. Blood seeped from his hair where a marble wing had grazed the scalp. He paid no attention to the scrape and the bite of oyster shells against his skin.

The blind man kept moving, laughing now with a low rumble that soared to a high-pitched titter. His pomaded hair was unusually long, twisted into curls in the back. Despite the moisture his suit looked crisp, hugging the narrow hips and flaring smoothly across the shoulders. Still laughing, he reached into his pants pocket and flipped something over his shoulder. It bounced and rang against marble facings as it fell to the path. Conall snatched at the shining thing and sighed with pleasure. Warm on his palm, it appeared to be a foreign coin, as large as a silver dollar—perhaps commemorative in purpose. On one side was a relief sculpture of a curly-haired king, a queen's profile visible behind his. The boy wondered if the blind man might have worn a crown in some alien region across the seas. It was possible, for the face on the coin had something in common with his.

Conall pillowed his head on one arm, waiting to see what the stranger with the flowers would do.

Far down the walk, he stopped and felt at the door of a tomb. He appeared to be tracing the inscription with his fingers. Satisfied that the place was right, he bent to place the flowers in an urn, delicately touching the petals as he arranged them. Going down on one knee in the sharp oyster shells, he bowed his head and placed a hand on the letters. He stayed that way for some minutes before getting up and moving slowly away, his tall black shape visible for some distance against the white blaze of tombs.

Afterward, Conall darted to the spot and touched the word engraved on the door as the man had done. Was it a woman's name? Was it his wife or someone else he had once loved? The sharp letter V was like a dagger under his fingertip. He imagined a tall, strong figure flushed with health. She would be powerful, like the blind man, able to slay rather than be slain. Briefly, with a faint sense of guilt, he thought of his mother and her ailing body. Perhaps the same disease had taken the woman that had turned the blind man's eyes to eggs. Perhaps she had died raging at the blackness that had robbed her of the bright world and the face of the man who was like a king. Perhaps he was nothing like a king but a thief who had stolen away with her to another country, like Lancelot with Guinevere.

He wanted to know, and of course wasn't able to tell. The odd name could have been merely a family name.

"Con!"

Doc had found him at last. The adventure in the white city of the dead was at an end.

Now back home in Cross Plains, Conall reached into his pocket and pulled out the coin, turning it absently between his fingers as the chains for the swing screeked and he pushed off from the porch rails. He had been unable to identify the country or the markings that looked a little like Greek, a little like runes. But it was a beautiful thing, the two bold faces in relief and the ship on the reverse that looked to him like Jason's *Argos*.

"Remember when we lived in Bagwell?" he said to his mother. "Remember when the ground was green from mold and the minnows and the fish swam past in the road? I remember lying in bed sick and seeing one jump on the other side of the panes."

"Yes," she said. "I remember when ugly black roses spotted the plaster, and the trunks of trees turned green and slick. Were you daydreaming just now? Did you hear me?"

"For he on honey-dew hath fed, / And drunk the milk of Paradise," Conall said, by way of an answer.

"Would you just look at that miserable pack of trash coming this way!"

She tapped her son on the arm, nodding toward the unpaved street where a knot of oilmen supported one of their own. Across the way, a couple of cowboys were half-dragging a friend. Coming along behind were two women propping up a third, who seemed to be suffering little more than hysterics, though a strip of ruffles had been torn from her dress and straggled behind her in the dirt.

"Son, get on in the house. And tell your father that he's got two, maybe three cash customers marching down the road."

"Yes'm," he said, though he didn't stop swinging until his mother repeated the request and then fell into a spasm of coughing.

Dropping the coin into his pocket, he got up, staring at the bruised, bleeding men and at the women in their flounced, deep-cut dresses. To him the whores in their gowns were beautiful, like spotted orchids—a vivid yellow, a peach, and a violet. He glanced uneasily at his mother, who was still dabbing at her mouth with a handkerchief. If she were a flower, it would be bloodroot, which blossomed and was gone so quickly that some called it *windflower*. All that remained were the leaves (even they died back early) and the white root with its bloody orange sap that could be either healing or poisonous and gave the plant its name. *Sanguinaria*. Once he had seen a picture in an open book at school. He didn't care so much about plants, but the vivid name on the page had stopped him.

"Get on with you," Maeve said, a foreign lilt creeping into her voice. "Ruffians and soiled women aren't our kind. Don't even look. Don't give those blackguards the satisfaction of notice. And don't ever forget that the blood of the old Irish kings and queens pours through your veins. Go and climb into the tangled branches of your family tree. In the fourteenth century, wasn't it our ancestors wore the beaten gold in their hair?"

The knotted interlace of a fabulous live oak spiraled up in his mind. Half red, half blue, the family tree was split like the colored drawings of veins and arteries in his father's anatomy books.

A maze of blood, he thought, *that holds me fast. Like a crooked root.*

The Blue Jars

"Why, cowboys were so tough in those days that they wore buffalo hide for smallclothes and barbed wire for belts—"

"You gentlemen will have to excuse me," Maeve said, coming into the kitchen where Doc Weaver was regaling a patient with stories, "but I must claim the kitchen. As a lady's prerogative," she added.

The doctor whipped his napkin onto the table.

"Conall likes my tales and jokes," he said, "and so do most other people. For a woman with a head full of poetry, you sure do have a gift for spoiling a fine story, Maeve."

"You'd do better to collect your fees, Dr. Weaver, than to entertain patients with scalawag adventures at my table," she said, lifting her chin, her voice cool. "You have an office in town, after all."

Whistling, the doctor reached for his hat and stood up. The other man, dressed in limp bib overalls and a long-sleeved shirt, didn't meet Maeve's eyes but ducked his head and trailed the doctor from the room.

She was breathing fast, the pulse at her throat fluttering. The kitchen was woman's territory again, and though much of the time Maeve didn't bother with a lot of cooking, she gave a small tight smile.

"He'll be out in his Model T, eating breakfast and noon dinner and supper with patients, joshing and telling coarse anecdotes," she muttered. "What's the point when a meal is just me and a boy of thirteen?" She frowned, appearing less than satisfied with her unspoken reply to this question. "Still," she said, "the kitchen is a wife's domain, and he has no right to go messing with sick people here, and leaving bloody bandages unspooled across the floor. Let him see visitors in the sitting room!"

She thumped a wooden spoon on the table.

Today Maeve would be canning, having bought a load of tomatoes from a local farmer. He had thought the things might just be his ticket to prosperity. In the end he did not find enough buyers or, more importantly, anyone who wanted to ship his produce east and north. In Boston and New York, there would be people to buy his crop. But the venture wasn't well planned, or else this wasn't quite the time for such enterprise. Plenty of people still had no idea what to do with a tomato, and they weren't likely to find out from him, it seemed.

The screen door banged.

"What's all this?"

"Just a whole lot of tomatoes," she called. "They're so lovely and red! I got them practically for free because they're about to go bad."

Conall came in the room, dog at his heel.

"And some ignorant people around here think they're not edible," she continued. "They're a hundred years behind the times."

"Was that our Model T?"

"Your father just left."

"This morning he asked me to ride up toward Caddo East. We were going to stop and look for fossils after he lanced an abscess. I've been wanting to go for a long time."

Maeve clanged several pots onto the stove top.

"He probably forgot about it. But that's all right," she told him. "You can help me."

"I could go wrestle and box with Fletcher," he said, voice plaintive, but didn't say more.

So he went to and from the pantry, carrying blue mason jars with wire bails. The dog now lay sleeping on the grass, occasionally cocking an ear when he heard a voice from inside. Maeve was telling stories about her ancestors, lighting now on Colonel Martin's silver mine and skirmishes with Apaches; now on the gold rush; now on the battles of Bedford Forrest; and now on an Irish hill crowned by a cairn. After a while her son began talking, too, lured by these familiar stories.

At dusk, jars stood on every surface in the shadowy kitchen, and the last two pots of tomatoes bubbled on the stove. Conall was ladling the tomatoes into jars, while his mother sat wiping her face on an apron printed with cups and saucers.

"I'm awful tired," she said, slumping in the chair. "I'll be glad to get done. I feel like water. Let's stop after you finish filling that one. And then I'll just throw some vegetables and a bone in the other pot and make soup. What a mess! You can help me clean up in the morning."

The boy didn't answer. He still wanted to wrestle or box, and he was remembering how his mother had prevented him from playing football at school. She was afraid he could get hurt, and she had settled it with his father so they both agreed. She didn't like boxing, either, or any kind of risk.

"You could go over to Fletcher's house," she said. "It's not too late. Almost, though. You'd best hurry."

A burden seemed to slip from him at her words. He would wrestle and box until they sent him home. *Yes!* That's what he would do. He began slopping tomatoes into the crock. He had been angry because his whole afternoon was gone, and it seemed his evening would be sacrificed on the altar of the tomato. And he probably wouldn't even like tomatoes!

Twilight made the blue glass of the jars seem to glimmer and darkened the contents. He looked around, wondering at how dusk could turn a place so dreamlike and weird.

"The kitchen looks like you've been canning blood," he said.

"Conall! What a terrible thing to say."

"It does," he persisted. "This could be a place where witches gather. Untamed women who dance under the moon on the plains. Perhaps this house was built on a site sacred to the Caddo Indians. Or maybe it's where somebody mysteriously vanished, only he hasn't really gone anywhere because he's been murdered."

"Eddie," she said, referring to her husband. A mischievous smile flicked across her face.

Conall, about to slip out the house and race to meet Fletcher, paused to fantasize about the murder.

"You would've dumped the victim in the outhouse, only you have a nice fixed-up home with an indoor bathroom," he said. "Marshal Pinkston and his men will come looking for him, and you'll give them leave to search. The marshal will take to you because you're such a refined and glamorous consumptive, probably a poet. These Texas lawmen are all secret poets. The pantry will look like just anybody's pantry, all beans and corn and pickles. Even poets have to eat. You'll look serene and sensitive and say how lucky you were to have gotten hold of so many fine red tomatoes."

A touch of gaiety came into her voice as Maeve repeated the words, *secret poets*. Her laughter wobbled slightly out of control, as if she were too tired to stop, and Conall joined in. But when she lifted the handkerchief to her mouth a small red rose bloomed on the cambric. The joke had spoiled itself.

Mother and son were silenced, exchanging a single glance.

Niannian

The dog's tail wagged as he jumped up and pawed Conall's legs. As one, they took off and raced to the edge of the back lot and swept along its border before dashing toward the house. The boy stooped to pick up the book he had left on the steps and then rushed into the kitchen, the dog slipping in at his heels before the screen door banged.

"Caradog is smarter than scads of people, Mama. He comes when I call, every time, except when he's eating, and even then he looks around to tell me that he's too busy."

"Cara's smart, all right. He's a nice creature. Look on the table. There's a slice of pear stack cake with cream cheese icing. One of your father's patients stopped by."

Conall sat down and dropped a few crumbs by his chair. Caradog nosed them experimentally and looked up, tail flicking.

"It's good," Conall whispered, reaching to let the dog lick icing from his fingers. He knew that his mother would have liked payment in cash. They couldn't settle the electric bill or buy his next pair of shoes with a cake.

Maeve cut herself a wedge and sat across from him. She slid his book across the table and opened it to the table of contents.

"You were reading this big hard history book about Genghis Khan? Fletcher's mama was telling me how startled she is by the words you know and all the history. You understand this stuff? You read a book about him before, didn't you?"

He nodded, mouth crammed with cake.

"I made up a story. At least I think so because sometimes what I make up feels real, and I can't tell whether it is or not—maybe I dreamed—about when I was a Mongol boy."

Pushing her plate to one side, his mother picked up a knife and continued nipping the tops from okra and cutting the pods into wheels. Now and then she paused to take another bite of pear cake.

"About when you were a Mongol boy." A smile quirked the corner of her mouth.

"In the tale I didn't have to go to school," he said. "I didn't have to wait till summer to have a durn life. Can I have more cake?"

"Conall, I'm sure you meant to say, 'May I, please?'"

He repeated the words and held out his plate.

"What did you do instead of school?" She cut a piece of cake with the vegetable knife, speckled with white okra seeds and streaked with sap from the pods.

"I played. There was a dog there, too, or maybe it was a pet fox. The men rode away to hunt and left you and me and my sister."

"You had a sister? I guess we didn't lose our baby, then. Not like here in Texas."

"We stayed in the ger most of the time, though I took my dog and bow and hunted in the mornings. Do you know what *ger* means?"

Maeve shook her head.

"A big round tent with ropes lashed around it. It looks just the same shape as the cake! Maybe you would remember, if this really happened," he said slowly, "or maybe you were too ill.

"My father had told me to look after our wood-and-copper totem, because you were sick, and not to offend it. Inside lived a powerful spirit. At night I could feel the totem's missing eye, burning like a star, watching me through the fire hole. It made me feel afraid of the night sky, even though my own light was out there, somewhere, sparkling. I thought maybe another boy at the ends of the earth might be pointing up and saying what a beautiful star the eye was, but somehow I was still afraid.

"An old woman stopped by the ger, bringing mutton and clotted cream as a present. One day I was surprised to find that she was your sister, because she had not said so. She had gone straight to your side and cried out, *Niannian!* She told us that one of your four souls must have been stolen by a spirit on a night when she had dreamed that her sister's star was dim."

Maeve paused from cutting more okra. "What does that mean? I have no earthly idea."

"It's simple," Conall said. "A dim star meant a weak windhorse, see, and that meant you were losing strength and power. Your star might go out, and you would die. I worried that it was my fault because our totem might have been offended by my dislike of his missing eye, but she said not to worry—the harm had come to you from outside this world. Near her own ger lived a powerful shaman, she told us, and he would be able to drive any evil spirit from your body. Tomorrow we would visit him. In the morning my sister and I saddled the bay horses—the best ones had gone with my father and older brothers, and I had to ride behind my old auntie, who stank of stale milk and juniper smoke. The dog-fox creature pattered after us, nosing at wild smells and dashing sideways when leaves blew. I didn't like going, even though wherever I went would be the center of the world for me, as it is for everyone. But not for you! You had slipped away from the place where each person must stand, and your star was growing cold."

"That sounds pretty bad for me," Maeve said.

"It was," Conall said. He pointed his fork at her. "It was very bad."

"How about a story where I'm strong and clever?"

"But that would be a different story," Conall said. His mouth was pleasantly crammed with cake, but he went on, and his mother forgot to scold him.

"Soon the crows sang out *kraaa!* in warning and lumbered up as we approached the spot where the body of our healer, Yadgan, was lashed high in a tree decorated with colorful strips of cloth. The trunk aimed toward the heavens like the world tree where all times and all places meet. Her hide skirt and bright hat and fan made of ribbons of gay silks had been left to the winds. Threads would turn up in nests of birds. As my auntie made an offering, the string that had held our shaman's prayer necklace broke, and beads pattered onto rotting leaves, where they lay like shining berries. One winked its light at me.

"'Yadgan,' I whispered. The last time I saw the *otoshi* alive, she had put the little reddish dog that looked like a fox—or the fox that looked like a dog—in my arms."

"That's a name? *Yadgan*?"

Conall ignored the question. "Nearby was a cairn. We walked around it three times to gain strength, and I helped you place a pebble on top."

"What was wrong with the mother—with me?" Maeve got up and spooned corn meal over the rounds of okra.

"A spirit had taken away one of your souls."

"Souls? Was the illness TB?"

"One part of the problem was something wrong with your body," Conall said. "The other part was spirit sickness. Mongols can't talk about one without the other."

Maeve stared at the okra sprinkled with yellow corn meal. "So I have—so I *had*—something wrong with my body, and a spirit sickness. Where does Genghis Khan come into all this?"

"Nowhere," Conall said. "I didn't meet him until later."

She laughed, and sat back down with a bushel basket of beans to string and snap.

"So do you want to hear the rest of the story?"

She snapped a bean into three lengths before nodding. "I guess so."

"Yadgan had been small and bent but with fire in her black eyes. She had always supported the women and was midwife to their babies. Wives were often left alone because of war or hunting, so Yadgan heard all their troubles and called them her beautiful little golden suns who burned on the hearth while men adventured on their bay horses, coming and going like the moon in the heavens."

"Women are the sun and men the moon," Maeve said, stopping with a bean lifted in the air. "That's odd. I like that."

"It took us many hours to reach the shaman. When Qasar saw us winding through the trees, he screamed. In the dusk, his ger looked as if the moon had drifted to earth and been tied down to keep it from floating back up. The man's headdress with antlers and his moon house made my skin creep."

"What did he do?" Maeve frowned. "I don't like screaming men."

"Hush, Mama," Conall said. "After calling for his helper to fetch a skin, the shaman drank milk that had steeped all day with a stone that had fallen from heaven.

"We crowded inside the ger with auntie's neighbors, but the shaman's ritual fan didn't blow away evil, and his gestures were useless. The people groaned in sympathy. Then an assistant brought mushrooms, rice mead, and a little house made of twisted grass—a cage for a spirit. Soon people began dancing in a circle, repeating the shaman's song and shouting as a drumbeat faltered or quickened.

"Lifting arms and legs as if to climb, he mounted the world tree. Though he straddled a staff and rode on his spirit journey, you remained spent and pale. He leaped around you, shooting a bow and arrow or slashing the air with a knife."

"That blustery fellow would give me a headache," Maeve said.

"Do you want to hear a story or not?" Conall held out his plate for another slice of cake.

"Go on," Maeve told him, cutting a piece. "It's pretty good cake, isn't it?"

"So," Conall said, "finally he crashed headlong onto the floor, twitching and moaning, and the helper dragged him from the fire's edge. The shaman had gone searching in the lower world for your soul, down in the depths where Erleg Khan rules."

"Who's he?"

Conall swallowed a bite of cake before he answered. "Lord of the lower world. He gave diseases to the world after his brother made humans."

"Don't think I like that one either," Maeve said. "I don't see any use in diseases. But keep going."

"Auntie herded my sister and me outside, where the dawn was beginning to snuff out the stars. The night had flown away while we were in the ger. But the *Altan Hadaas*, the pole-star nail that holds the heavens fast, still shone. We were damp with sweat. I shook in the chill as my auntie faced away from sunrise and the dangerous sky spirits that bring illnesses. She looked toward the kindly sky spirits, and she blessed the mighty eternal Heaven. The little fox-dog padded over and curled against my feet. I was sorry because everyone knows that a fox crossing from left to right is unlucky—and though he wasn't quite a fox, just then he looked unlucky."

Conall stopped, scraping the crumbs from his plate.

"I could eat another," he said, knowing that she would refuse if he asked for a fourth piece.

Maeve ignored the hint. "So what happened?"

"I don't remember any more." He tapped the plate gently with his fork. "When I'm a man, I'll eat four pieces of cake."

"You'll get fat," Maeve warned. "So you don't know whether I—or she—lived or died."

"No. That's all of the story I know."

At some point, Maeve had paused in her stringing and snapping. Now her hands were relaxed, folded atop the mound of beans.

She leaned forward, scrutinizing his face.

"Where did you get all of that?"

"Sometimes when I read in a book, I remember, or I feel like I remember," he said. "Sometimes I get glimpses, like the red dog or the meteorite in the milk, and I don't know where they came from. Maybe I read them and forgot. Sometimes I think it's all Texas— Mongolia's just like the Indians' medicine men and their tipis, with braves riding to hunt or to battle and leaving the women to rule. Other times I feel sure that I have lived it all, and one long memory pours out." Conall picked up the plate as if he might lick it, hesitated, and then put it down again.

"You certainly didn't learn that business about souls in Sunday School," she said, giving him a sharp look.

"But there's some that's not so different," he told her. "The eternal blue sky the Mongols call *Tenger Etseg* is above everybody and everything. Everything comes from Father Sky, joined with Mother Earth. Tenger's not a person but has sons and daughters. Tenger has a creator son, Ulgen Tenger. And a devilish son, Erleg Khan. Everybody has a little fragment of Tenger in the crown of his head. Spirit and strength flow from the upper world and reach inside the soul."

Maeve picked up a fistful of beans and began stringing them. "Isn't that curious? Fletcher told me that you're always telling wild tales to your school friends."

"They ask for them," he said. "Mostly they like yarns about pirates and explorers or about cowboys and Indians."

"Och, and isn't that like a boy?" A faint Irish lilt had crept into her voice.

"Yeah," he said, "it is. I like them, too."

"That story you just told reminded me of 'Kubla Khan.'"

He smiled, aware that this was a very high compliment, coming from his mother. She liked to recite poems, but that one remained her favorite.

Boomtown

Conall smacked steadily at the bag with his gloves.

The high whine of insects, the two-noted song of a distant train, and his voice provided the only other sounds. He was talking out his ideas about characters, his words jerky, blurted-out.

"They grow—just like a plant—a fierce—wild man out of the moors—blue tattoos out of the forest shadows—a lonely hunter out of the Eastern—forests—a hard—indomitable—man out of rocks."

To end with a new idea and a burst of fireworks as he battered the bag into submission and let out a few war whoops was an intense pleasure. One of the neighbors was watching him as she pegged clothes onto the line. Conall shrugged and, tossing away his gloves and grabbing a pair of flat irons, dashed from the yard. He wouldn't look at the condemnation in her eyes. At fifteen he was tired of being called strange for reading a book while he waited for his father at a patient's house or for shadow-boxing with an imaginary opponent as he walked to town or for knowing a word that somebody else didn't and thought fancy—fancier than any word had the right to be in Cross Plains. The woman had mocked him for acting out a story as he wrote, the windows open and his shouts audible from her front porch. Misbegotten dolts! His dog had more sense. Barking, Caradog leaped out of the shadows and into the bright sunlight. Conall called to him but kept running. Before long, he would be stronger than anybody at school, so nobody could ever hurt him again. He wouldn't be afraid of the roughnecks and bullies of the town anymore because he would be able to handle himself against anyone.

Soon he had passed the outlying houses and taken shelter by a heap of stones meant for a house that had never been built. He pushed the irons up slowly and then slowly lowered them. Caradog sat down at his feet, watching eagerly. When he got bored, Conall picked up slabs of rock and hefted them overhead.

"Caradog, you old pup pirate," he said, pausing to give him a hug. The dog jumped up and licked his face. "This is our lair, with the secret buccaneer's treasure under the dead king's haunted barrow where no one will ever find it—no one will dare to look."

"Wonder what kind of man I'll be," he said, continuing his earlier thoughts. "The old heroes grew out of their land like olive trees on a hillside or acanthus in a Roman meadow. But I come out of a place with an infinite sky that makes even a silo into a stub and dominates the flat land. It's like trying to be born out of nothing. I come out of the wind's whistle, out of the rattle of dry oak leaves, out of tumbleweed roamers that don't stop somersaulting over the world. Maybe that means I'll never belong."

"Hey!"

"Fletcher! You made it."

Conall tackled his friend and pinned him to the ground. When Fletcher yelled *uncle*, the boys laughed and flopped back on the hot earth.

"Let's go to town," Fletcher proposed.

"My mother wants me to quit going to the stores without her."

"Why?"

"She says that the oil boom has made the whole place unsafe. Too many cannibal hogs at the trough, I guess. But I'm old enough to watch out for myself."

"She doesn't want to cast her dear little pearl to the swine," Fletcher said. He jumped to his feet, offering to spar. The boys scuffled, throwing a few jabs, as the dog leaped around them, barking. But the thought of town had cast its lure over them.

"Come on," Conall said. "I wouldn't mind taking a gander at the magazines at the drugstore."

Fletcher was still thinking about the boom that had swollen the town. "You got to keep your money close. And better not hang out your britches, either. Did you hear that the Groves had their clothes stripped off the line, right down to the diapers?"

Conall tucked the two irons into a hiding place among the stones.

"At least they kept what they were wearing, unless the thief had mighty clever fingers."

"I heard that Mrs. Grove was in her nightgown and sent a shirt-tail kid next door to borrow a dress and that later on she spent a bundle at Higgenbotham's."

The boys sauntered along the road, chunking stones into the weeds while Caradog rooted through scrub, flushing birds and chasing scents of mice and rabbit.

The desultory conversation was pleasing to Conall, though a portion of his mind was set on his earlier imaginings. Restless barbarians roamed his inner plains, clambered up and over the rocks, and strode along the edge of the ditch.

As they neared the Racket Store, the road crumbled, gouged from too much use—too many mules and wagons, too many automobiles, too many horses. The boys leapfrogged over fissures in the ground.

"Claw marks," Conall called. "The spurred demon dragon of the secret Caddo cave flew this way."

"Quagmires of the damned!" Fletcher ducked as his friend tossed a clod of dirt at his head.

Cars puttered by, one backfiring, another fishtailing to a stop.

"Cara, stay close!" Conall gave a short, high-pitched whistle that brought the dog to heel.

A gang of roughnecks brushed past the boys, jostling them into the corrugated street. They were oilmen done for the day, still clad in soiled work pants or coveralls. Swerving to pass a woman in an emerald silk dress, they whistled and raised their caps and jeered at one another. Conall put his hand out to grasp the post in front of a store. The knot of men, the provocative smile, the brilliant dress seemed to echo another scene long ago or perhaps rose from some male tribal memory, tattooed in his genes. History and legends swam around him, unsettled his hold on the raw Texas town. The cloudy face of Vortigern drifted across the blaze of sky. Commands from Crusaders swirled around his head, and Genghis Khan galloped by in a puff of Model-T exhaust. Conall looked around, wondering if anyone else had noticed. Had he once been knocked aside by some group of warriors intent on a courtesan? He had lived lives in every corner of the Roman Empire and in each one had struggled to throw off the yoke of authority and the demands of women—or so he had dreamed, bent over a book in the bedroom that had once been a porch.

He heard a shout: "Howdy, Doc!"

"There's your daddy, being toadied-to by the village layabouts," Fletcher said, pointing to where Doc Weaver was being mobbed by admirers, one of whom was vigorously pumping his arm.

"He loves the boom," Con said, pausing to watch. "Likes being the town doc and general raconteur, and believes we'll get as rich as Croesus if we only put money on the right damn derrick. I can tell you now that's not likely. He'll be there half an hour, spewing out stories, because there's not much he relishes more than an audience."

"Important fellow when the oilman gets clobbered by a spar or a cowboy gets thrown," Fletcher said.

"With the oilmen and the cowboys, it's mostly just fights. He makes a few dollars every week from stitching up cuts. Talks their ears off while he sews. You know, he's a good tale-spinner—one of the best." Conall thought of his mother and felt a twinge of regret. Somehow he couldn't praise his father without the sense that he was being disloyal.

Outside the Racket Store, a clerk was setting boards across the mud and potholes, dashing in and out of traffic as he threw down the warped lumber and kicked it into place. A stream of young women in zingy, zinnia-colored dresses began teetering across the street in high heels, gasping and shrieking and tossing their heads to attract attention. One balanced with her arms out as though navigating a narrow log bridge over a stream, her showy net shawl of green and silver fluttering like useless wings.

Coming the other way was a sooty urchin holding a lit sparkler, seemingly entranced by the light and looking neither to the left nor right. In front of a nearby store, a hawker sang out:

Get your Wonder Candles,
Safe with spark-shield handles—
Star-frizzles,
Light-sizzles:
Mark my cry,
Come and buy!

Cars backed up or veered to avoid gulfs in the road, bucking across the broken-up maze of boards laid down for pedestrians. Meanwhile a fresh party of automobiles roared in from out of town with a great sputtering fuss, accompanied by the blare and tootle of horns and popping noises like the firing of half-penny strings of firecrackers.

Standing on a crate, a homegrown preacher exhorted an audience made up of a jeering rowdy and a small barefoot child. In an unexpected instant of astonishing, angelic silence, one line clanged on the ears of passersby: *Claiming to be wise, they became fools, and exchanged the glory of the immortal God for images resembling mortal man or birds or animals or reptiles.* Then a horse reared and whinnied, and a cowboy sawed at the reins, cursing and choking, his chaw catapulted with great force into the roadway, where it was run over by a delivery wagon. Six or seven cats streaked from under a porch, yowling as if all the imps of hell had been clamped onto their tails. A mother clutching a squalling baby and towing a child abruptly fled across the street in the wake of the bright moving rainbow of harlots, her shoes clattering on freshly laid planks.

Conall hooked a finger around his dog's homemade collar. "You ever seen a picture of a termite nest ripped open, how they rush around, gathering up the grubs?"

"Hello, sugar." A woman in a sulphur yellow dress flounced past, leering at them from a face painted with cochineal lips and cheeks and jet eyelashes as thick and bold as wheel spokes.

"Hel-lo," Fletcher said. Leaning over, he whispered, "I think she liked me."

Conall snorted. "You and every other two-bits-to-spend dunce."

His eyes rested on the girl in the wake of the yellow whore—delicate and almost pretty, if she hadn't been tarted up with rouge—the poor thing looked scared, scurrying to keep up, and seemed to be hiding behind her older friend. Perhaps the woman in yellow was her own mother! Soon enough the pale young girl would be prancing about, he imagined, shaking her slender wares at the dance hall.

The scurrying ant-bed town with its wild-western trash seemed to Conall like a lively painted screen laid over something inhuman. What if behind all these painted or sunburned faces were others, uglier and less familiar? He already suspected that no one here would be friendly to his dreams. In the post office they had laughed when he had brought his first story in to be mailed—as if anything worthwhile could come out of the Cross Plains region!

Behind the harlot's mask and the finely tucked yellow gown might be the intricately fitted skin of a rattlesnake. The oilmen, mad with lust to be rich, could be coiled copperheads writhing in a den. Card sharks and addicts might lie looped in the sun, jaws flopped open to show the smooth white lining and fangs, waiting for an innocent foot to pass.

Even the word hawkers had failed him. Schoolteachers with their regimens and their do's-and-don'ts written in fancy script with colored chalk on the blackboard had earned his scorn. They had bored him from his first day at school, when he who could read and knew poems by heart had to sit on a hard bench, fuming inwardly against the teacher, and recite the alphabet. The other children hadn't minded. Most of the other boys his age cared about nothing but games and fighting at recess. He had felt apart from them all, though he made friends after settling down in Cross Plains. What did he have but Fletcher and a few other cohorts from school, his parents, and Caradog?

"I've always hated rattlesnakes," he murmured, "but at least they show a true face and signal before they strike."

Birth at Caddo Peak East

Sandstone crumbled between his fingers, making the raw skin smart where he had cut himself.

"You're a beauty, aren't you?"

Conall scooped a fossil shell from its sleeping place and plucked up something that looked like the curled spray of a fern, though it was hard to say—might be the body of some feathery sea animal.

His cap was heavy with fossils, as were his pockets, and his pants were powdered with dust. He had intended to bring a bucket but had gone off without it—so deep in his book that he didn't know it was time to leave until his mother knocked on the window that separated her bedroom from his and called to him that his father was sounding the horn.

"Long ago, Caradog, the Eocene sea washed over the Caddo Peaks," he said, "and strange monsters swam and bright worms wriggled."

Caradog thumped his tail, sending up a puff of fine rock flour.

For the last fifteen minutes, Conall had been declaiming his own poetry to the dog, but now his thoughts went to the tale he was working on. He was sixteen, and though he had been sending out stories for a year, not a one of them had sold. Yet.

From the distance of the road, his figure might have seemed to be praying as he bent over the fossils. The truth was that he had begun telling a story in his usual way, ranting and sometimes gesturing, fishing for the unknown at the end of a line of words. But he went on moving the fossils, fiddling with their arrangement as if they might help him think and invent.

Conall always found the mountains inspiring—two ancient seabed landmarks that had been thrust higher than any ground close by.

"We could be archaeologists, Caradog," he said, "and find a haunted sword from the Crusades or unearth a mummy gripping the cursed treasure of Ramses or discover the tomb of Merlin."

He scraped at the sandy dirt with a chunk of ironstone, gripped by the idea of being a treasure hunter. Oh, he had stacked his fresh finds into weird towers of spikes and shells, but surely there was more than these easy pickings—a better dream than fossils. Then, barely an inch down, he discovered an ebony surface, cold on his fingertips.

Whooping, he redoubled his efforts. Even the dog joined in, kicking the grit into a storm. Before long, a black torso was partially uncovered and then legs and the tops of leather boots. Last of all, Conall carefully brushed pebbles from the lean face and swept away the powder that sealed the mouth. The features had been hidden from the sun so long that they were as bloodless and waxy as those of a corpse, the skin looking blanched next to the jet hair. The dry lids lifted jerkily, revealing irises of blue ice. The figure was still encased by earth, and seemed as helpless as a butterfly half-sealed in the chrysalis.

"It's about time you called for me," he said in a voice as stern as stone and as weary as the long ages since rapier-thin fish hunted for green minnows in the shallows of the Caddo sea. "I've been a useless instrument and a sword rusted in its scabbard while the world has worsened. Evil laid its cables under the oceans and pierced remote corners that could have been peaceful, if only the devil had stayed away."

The fossil star in the boy's hand crumbled between clenched fingers. He didn't notice the car below on the road or the figure waving.

"I've been manacled in the earth, dreaming of a day of blood and vapor with the fire of the sun gone nightmare black and the moon stained crimson." Silt streamed from the hair as the partly buried man forced his shoulders upward, ramming the sides of his prison.

Conall didn't try to help. He kneeled, gazing into the harsh, terrible face as visions woke in him.

"Look there! Again these eyes rake across the vulture sky where birds wearing the corrupt faces of men wheel, armed with the poisonous talons of dragons that lashed their ungainly way out from the primordial ooze." He stared at the wings, his face set in a mask that signaled vengeance and retribution. "Since the raising of this peak, I have been biding the day of my release. Around me slumber the white fossils of creatures that were monstrous in their hungry innocence, but they are pure next to the disease-gnawed bones of evil men, feculent to the marrow. The world has been whirling in the dark since Adam's teeth broke the skin of the apple. I have come to say that wrong and sin and suffering shall not rule all the iron waste lands of this earth forever, that evening shall not always whisper vileness to the morning and kiss her auroral lips with slimy teeth that stink of murder and decaying flesh!"

From the road came a persistent noise of honking, which Conall put firmly out of mind.

Rock shattered as a fist broke through to the air.

Closing his eyes, the man gathered his strength and began to pray. "God of my people—God of my time that is not this time but another—inscrutable, unknowable—God of my Puritan tribe—God who made this boy who is the dreamer of me—God from whom all comes and all streams back-to in mystery—keep me from cursing this day and my destiny—set me ablaze against men who are devils and against the dark powers and the evil principalities of the cosmos—stop my mouth from blaspheming this world, I who am the scourge for demons and the avenger of the helpless. Give me strength, God of the mountain summits and the winding caves, to witness the mangled sufferings of this people and to slash my way through all labyrinths of jungle or stone or blood to the still, unbeating heart of silence where the ungovernable powers wait."

Another fist jammed against the soft rock. The caping of stone on his shoulders quaked and shed motes and flakes onto the black chest.

A horn sang out three notes, ending with a squawk.

Conall stood, casting a glance over his shoulder.

With one mighty shove, the man thrust himself upward, sitting up in the throne of his grave and precipitating a cataract of shards from his back and shoulders. In another instant he jerked unsteadily to his feet while avalanches of powder rolled from his body. When he reeled, the shrieks of the circling hawks plucked at the sky.

"At last I am born, even if it be under the shadows of a curse," he shouted, shaking his fist at the ragged wings.

He turned his curiously light eyes on his liberator, raised his rawboned limbs to the heavens, and began to prophesy.

"Boy, your mouth is over-tender, and those eyes under the thick brows look likely to weep. Locked in the jail of your days and place, you are a solitary like me and buried deep. The sandstone seals your trembling lips, the grave encases you so that you cannot stir, and the traces of ages past kiss your forehead and brand you with the grief and painful joy of lives that flashed out of the fount and then fell back into the pool, aeons ago. I, the man born of rock and the oracle of doom, prophesy to my own sublunary maker and say, *This day you are born again with me. But if you will not burst your bonds and wander freely in the world, you will die of the encasing stone and the dust in your mouth!*"

Conall stumbled, dropping the fossil in his hand. A fierce exhilaration pressed against him. He imagined it sending infinite fine cracks through a mass of mind-forged mountain that held him in its fastness.

"Name me, boy!"

The swordsman was a macabre figure. Grains sifted from his clothes, and dust swirled around his body. Only the gaze seemed wholly untouched by earth and stone. It too struck Conall as otherworldly, like an alien light emitted from a place of rocks where druids once marched, carrying a ball of foxfire in one hand and branches of mistletoe in the other. The name sprang forth from his mouth like a sword from the stone.

"You are—Fitzcain!"

The man prisoned him with a blue glacial stare and at last nodded.

"So let it be. The name is good, though ruthless," he said, "and I will not object to slaying my own brother, should he need slaying. Such is my fate, to wander and to punish and to assist those who are trodden by boot and wheel. I accept the sign of Cain."

The horn set up an incessant honking.

When it ceased, Conall turned his head reluctantly and saw another rigid figure—his father marching through the faraway scrub.

"Come on, Caradog! Somebody's going to be after my scalp if we don't hurry—maybe even if we do."

Clutching the hat sagging with fossils against his chest, Conall launched himself down the slope. He was out of breath, as though he had been running a long way, but he waved and called hoarsely, "I'm coming."

Once he jerked his head back and glimpsed a whirlwind of dust, barely visible against the pale sky.

The Soul, the Spirit, and the Meteor

The incident of the child's soul, the Spirit of Story, and the meteorite was said to be a tale that Conall Weaver recounted in his last year of high school, living away from Cross Plains and just about as close to happy as he would ever be. The recollections of friends agree that Conall had been telling stories all one afternoon. The boys had been lying on the floor at full-length, glad for the coolness of the boards on a hot day while they drew a battle scene with pencils on a long, smudged roll of paper. They were drinking sugared mint water, one of them occasionally pressing a glass with its cool gathered drops against a forehead or arm. Somebody asked for a story about pirates, and Conall dreamed up a fresh installment in the adventures of Long-slake, who plied his trade in a scribbled path from Singapore to the Ivory Coast. The tale of Long-slake and the Horse Pirates involved much scurrying up ropes, a lot of dashing about decks with swords, and the attempted rescue of an unexpectedly feisty damsel. The Texas plains being entirely too hot and dry for pirates, the boys relished the story and called out encouragement to Long-slake in his watery troubles.

Afterward, Conall rolled onto his back and, staring at the plaster ceiling, told a little tale that ended only when Maeve came in, fagged with heat, the handkerchief that they all knew to be spotted with blood balled in a fist. Unlike most of his stories told to please friends, this one featured himself. Perhaps that is why the boys—then young men with jobs and wives or sweethearts—recalled it in later days after Conall had departed the world so decisively.

Evidently it was a mark of their respect for his storytelling that the boys wanted to know whether the tale was true. While they put final touches on the drawing, tossed pencils into a box, and then admired and rolled up the battle scene of warriors with axes and dragon-decked shields and enemy heads freed by the sword, they argued about whether such things were possible. In the end, they leaned toward a yes. For some people. For Conall. Perhaps such easy trust in what seems impossible was only the sign of an age more ready and able to run and find the very roots of story, eager to hear revelations of a Grendel or a Faerie Queene or of the fair trees along a shining river, each one with leaves for the healing of the nations. Whatever the reason, the boys thought about Conall's words long enough to recall the day and the tale more than a decade later.

The story went something like this....

Once a meteor tunneled through the atmosphere and thumped into the earth, and as it fell, the boy Conall tumbled like Lucifer out of safety and lit rooms and into the deep night outside the house, where there were no streetlights and nothing but dark and more dark, like the infinite night folded and tucked inside a magician's top hat. The soul of the child was knocked clean from his body and flew like a bird into a soapberry tree and perched, shuddering at the shock and at the strangeness of seeing its own husk lying in the grass and weeds. Then with a flick of the wings, the soul shot toward the streak of light.

The bright flash was the mark left by the meteor. This stone traveler had passed a long way through nurseries of stars and precincts of space that were as empty and metaphysically maze-like as a desert. With hard knocks, it may have collected crystalline wisdom along the way, or perhaps the meteor was never anything but blank mineral sleep without dreams.

The bird-like curl of soul lit on the shoulder of a spirit who rode that bucking mustang meteor from the outback of space to the solid ground of Texas. And there on a pinhead of time, all the angels could have danced and told the epic tale of creation. Because much happened to Conall in that jot of time.

The Spirit—for she was the spirit of all story and all story-telling—laughed with pleasure and said to the soul of the boy, "Conall, little Conall Weaver, weave me a tale."

But the soul trembled and never said a word as the Spirit of Story flickered from one form to another, transforming from crouching mother to mighty athlete with upended, burning clouds of hair to girl made of thready light.

The Spirit, who seemed composed of flame and energy, laughed at the soul's silence. His shoulders (for just then the Spirit of Story was he) erupted into wings of fire that bathed the soul in light but did not burn its quiet, milky substance. The figure shifted his fire-feet and jigged on the hot surface of the meteorite.

"Did I tease you, little Conall? I am not sorry because I am never sorry, though I will give you a gift all the same. I will make you a maker, and you may be powerful, if you will," the Spirit of Story promised. "You will weave, Conall Weaver. You will travel until borders are nothing to you and your brogans and dancing boots are worn to pieces. You will be a hero, a conqueror, a defeated warrior, a boxer, a defender of faith, a king struggling against a tidal crash of barbarians from over the sea."

The child's soul answered in a voice like petals made of gold that clash lightly when tossed by the breeze. Who knows what the soul said? Yet perhaps the Spirit of Story knew, for he went on as if in reply.

"You will know people of many kinds, many countries. You will even travel to worlds that do not exist or once existed or do not yet exist, though such forays are a tricky thing for flesh and blood."

The soul of small Conall Weaver sighed with a drawn-out, burnished sound as if the gold petals were pinched between thumb and forefinger and then rubbed slowly together.

"Yes," the Spirit of Story cried, "you will go to those worlds, and you will know that this world is purely imaginary, a maze without a center, and that all the things you see are likewise imaginary. You will know that even your blood ties are illusory and passing. For everything inside a story—and know this most of all, that the world is a story and began with a word—is made up. And so the tale of a Green Knight with his chopped-off head still holding a knight of the Round Table to promises made is no less true than the tale of a man crammed with secrets who spontaneously combusts and leaves behind only a black, tallowy mark on the floorboards, and his story in turn is no less true than the tale of a Texas sharecropper's wife who has had a miscarriage only ten days before but just this morning was walking behind the mule and guiding the jerking plow."

The soul moved to and fro on the bright figure's shoulder and nudged against her slender neck, seeking a place out of the rush of air.

"Because," the Spirit of Story said, "this world is only a skip and a blink away from a more real one that you may find, or not, depending on how you walk and where."

This idea seemed to excite her so that her hair grew long and blood-colored and was swept into a glory by the breeze as the meteor plunged. (Still, all this was carved into one moment and monument of time, just as many tiny Indian elephants are carved and hidden in a small red bean as if they were seeds. Given the right soil and story, that bean could be the magic to grow a world of elephants.)

"Nothing is as it seems to be," she called out as the soul crept in the form of a milky bird along her arm. "Nothing! Always there is another story and another, tucked behind the arras of the world."

For a moment the Spirit of Story shifted to become a muscular man again before transforming into a woman who had something of Maeve's bent, hurt posture. She snatched up the soul and cupped it in her palm.

"I am a teller and will make you a story, Conall Weaver," she said in a voice that crackled with laughter. "I will make your life into a story to be remembered. And when you are dead and flown, you will not fathom if you have made your own tale or whether you are simply mine and all your days told by me. Though perhaps neither of those things will be true, and the secret is something else entirely."

The soul stirred in the nest of the Spirit of Story's hand. The curled fingers were no shelter from the burning thorn-fire of the voice and the fury of winds that fell so fast, so far....

As with a slap, the child's soul was shoved back into the body, and Conall lay on the ground, his eyes wide to the stars and his ears open to the cries of men running through the dark. He didn't breathe. He was like an empty bottle tossed into weeds.

Then he woke to the largeness of the sky and the flung expanse of stars. Breath choked him into life. He drank at the air, dragging it into his lungs. His fingers trembled and pushed against the skein of mosquito netting around his head and torso.

His uncle's face materialized between the boy and the stars, and a voice was asking. Conall couldn't answer. He was packed with words but couldn't speak, and so the uncle thrust him through the window and into the bed and the bald light of the bedroom.

Conall lay on the sway-backed bed, staring at the bare bulb burning at the end of a cloth-bound wire. A cheap pull-chain of tiny metal beads hung down. A dull yellow tape peppered with flies flapped once and hung still.

Outside, the men went on running and shouting, and once he heard a woman scream.

He was too small to lie there thinking that the world was imaginary, or that a truer world might lie behind this one. Instead, Conall remembered the stars sparkling on the sticky black tape of the sky and stared for a long time at the flies dangling from the ceiling. His eyes moved slowly away from their strange, dead constellations and rested on cracks that resembled the big, hand-drawn map of Maeve's family tree that she had unrolled to show him before they left home. Someone long before had marked the faded crowns of kings and queens on leaves distant from his own new leaf, added in lately by his mother with vermilion ink, a leaf unlike all the others. Conall stared up until the cracks were no longer a tree but a map showing a snarled, complicated river with many streams leading toward uncharted lands.

After a while, he closed his eyes, though he could still see the glow from the bulb through his eyelids. It smoldered like a red star. Until he sighed and let go of all that had happened and dropped like a stone into night and sleep, he thought only of a red sun lighting the river, a tangled maze that led Conall on and on into the world of dreams.